The
Twice Dead Groom

A Lou Rizzo Noir Mystery

By
George Mazzeo
High Flight Publishing
Gainesville, Florida
September 2020

Books by the Author

The Kellogg and Watt Aviation Thriller Series

Chasing Dragons
The Last Rajah

The Lou Rizzo Noir Detective Series

Rizzo's Rules
The Twice Dead Groom

For those who fight the good fight.

Chapter 1

Roz was hard at work when I arrived at the office, if you consider chain-smoking *Camels* and reading *True Detective* work. I didn't even rate a glance as she handed me the morning edition of the *Globe.* It's not difficult to know when she's put-out with me.

"Coffee's ready; been ready for two hours," she said.

"Alarm didn't go off," I offered in my defense.

"You might want to get a new one."

"It works occasionally."

"The same can be said of you."

Sometimes, it's hard to figure out who's in charge around here. I like to think I am, but I also like to think I'm Phillip Marlowe or Sam Spade. That's an oh-for-three in the box score.

"How about a shot of whiskey with that coffee, just to get the juices flowing."

Roz was the gatekeeper for the single bottle of Jim Beam we kept in the office to entertain clients.

"You know the rules, no booze before five," she said, "and you can forget that flask you hid in your washroom tank yesterday. I poured it down the drain."

"Second this week," I winced.

"Third," she replied. "Why don't you just give up and follow the rules?"

I'm a partially reformed drunk. I still drink too much but tell myself I've got it under control. Like most drinkers, I'm a good liar.

"The name on the door says Louis Rizzo, Private Investigator," I reminded her. "I get to make the rules."

"Sure, boss. Whatever you say."

I rolled my right eye. Only a crater remains under the patch where my left one used to be. I lost it while flying a B-25 in New Guinea back in '43. We got jumped by a flight of Zeros. They shot us up pretty good, almost killed me. There have been plenty of days I wish they had. My dream of a civilian flying career was over. Not much of a demand for one-eyed pilots. There were plenty around with standard equipment. I turned to the bottle for solace. I haven't found it yet, but I'm still looking. I'm sure it's at the bottom of one of them.

I spent years drowning in an ocean of self-pity, barely keeping my head above water by doing low-rent private eye work. Then, I went under. My choice was simple: sink or swim. I started slowly paddling towards sobriety a year ago. I've still got a few strokes to go before I reach the shore.

I tapped the newspaper.

"Anything interesting?"

"Check the front page. Murder at a society wedding."

"One of the guests?"

"The groom."

"That's one way to get out of it," I quipped.

She put down her magazine and gave me a disapproving look.

"That supposed to be funny? Get this; the minister asked the congregation if there were any objections to the union. Apparently, there was because the groom took a .30-06 in the back. Dropped him like a sack of potatoes. Probably not the storybook wedding the bride had in mind. Talk about getting left at the altar."

"Cops grab the shooter?"

"Read the article," she replied and turned her attention back to *True Detective.*

I opened the door to the inner office and tossed the paper on my desk. I grabbed my chipped coffee mug, it still had yesterday's grounds in the bottom, and headed back to the outer office. The coffee pot sat on a hot plate on our lone filing cabinet. I poured a cup, sat down my desk, unfolded the newspaper, laid it in front of me, and took a sip. The stale black liquid looked like motor oil and tasted like it was brewed from the brown waters of the Mississippi flowing just to the east.

"Coffee's awful," I called out.

"Tasted fine two hours ago."

I shook my head and directed my attention to the *Globe.* The headline splashed across the upper fold: *Gunned Down at Altar.* The byline was Dorothy Drake, the society page editor. Her flowery style was ill-suited for reporting on a murder.

The much-anticipated nuptials of Mercedes Miller, daughter of lumber baron Patrick Miller, and dashing financier Victor Jansen at Riverfront Christian Church came to a shocking and bloody conclusion when the groom was gunned down in cold blood.

A single shot rang out immediately after the minister, Reverend Chester Fletcher, had queried the crowd for objections to the proposed union. The shot came from the rear of the church. All eyes turned as one in that direction, leaving the minister as the only witness facing the groom. According to Fletcher, Mr. Jansen did not turn when the report rang out but rather, glanced down, studying the rapidly blossoming crimson rosette on his starched white shirt. The victim reached for the wound with his right hand and examined the blood on his fingers. He looked at Reverend Fletcher who described the victim's expression as one of confusion. He blinked once and lunged for his beloved.

The bride unleashed a chilling scream as her would-be mate clutched her and slid to the floor, leaving a trail of blood on her Parisian-designed, duchess satin gown. The stain ran from the sweetheart neckline through the high-fitted waist and down the A-line skirt to the floor.

Her wailing redirected the crowd's attention to the altar. Recognition led to panic, the church doors were thrown open and the attendees spilled into the street, the killer, no doubt, among them. The bride's father rushed to the altar and led his weeping daughter to an adjacent anteroom.

Police Commissioner Edward Holliman, among the distinguished guests, ably took command of the situation until his subordinates could respond. The case was handed off to Lieutenant William Newton who arrived on the scene fifteen minutes later.

Lt. Newton conducted a preliminary investigation and provided the following meager details: The single, *fatal shot came from the choir loft where police found its only occupant, the organist, unconscious. A suspected murder weapon, an Army surplus M-1, was found on the scene along with an empty vile of ether and a handkerchief soaked in the fluid. A single expelled casing was found on the floor along with a canvas sack. Police speculate that the sack was used to conceal the murder weapon allowing the assassin to secret it into the church. The organist, Mrs. Abigail Clayborn, was transported to a local hospital and will be questioned when she regains her wits. There are currently no suspects and no known motive. Commissioner Holliman has stated that no stone will be left unturned bringing the cowardly murderer to justice.*

The article was accompanied by the couple's engagement photo, one of the blood-stained bride leaving the altar with her father, and a third of a woman identified as Abigail Clayborn being carried off on a stretcher, her lace-gloved hands crossed on her chest in a death-like pose.

I put down the paper and took another swig from my cup. Today was my lucky day. It was a lucky day for anyone not named Bill Newton. He was a good cop and a stand-up guy. We worked a few cases and downed a few in the process. He was rough around the edges and didn't mind stepping on toes. He'd never see Captain, but he was a damn good detective for a flatfoot. He had a reputation for solving the toughest cases, so the brass kept him around. Plus, if things went sour, he made an excellent fall-guy, a fact he was shrewd enough to know and cynical enough to ignore.

Chapter 2

"What do you think?" asked Roz.

She was leaning against the door frame, right leg over left, cigarette in hand. She wore a black skirt and gray blouse. Her wavy blonde hair was worn shoulder-length framing intelligent, wide-set blue eyes above high cheekbones. Well north of plain and just south of beautiful, she had a worldly air about her that made her sexy. A guy could do a lot worse. She made it clear, on several occasions, I wasn't that guy.

Her family sent her East to college to find a suitable husband. None of the potential suitors measured up. She found them wanting, all cast from the same mold. They wanted her to host their cocktail parties, bear their offspring, and wash their BVDs. She was looking for something more. Her parents were sorely disappointed when she returned four years later with just a sheepskin.

She majored in philosophy and minored in literature. Upset their investment didn't turn out well, her family cast her out on her own. She found out the hard way that no one was willing to pay her to think great thoughts, so she scraped out a living doing clerical work at a bank. It only took a few trips around the bases for her to get bored with that.

Last year, I came into some inheritance money when my best friend was murdered. I never felt right about spending his dough, but it wasn't doing him any good where he was, so I pushed the guilt aside and spent some. I decided to add a little class to my private investigation agency, which I had been running out of the front seat of a '39 DeSoto. I rented modest offices and placed an advertisement for a Girl Friday. Roz answered. She was my first interview and I hired her on the spot. She was smart, educated and would dress up the place...best of all, she came cheap. The attitude came later, but that was mostly for show. You know what they say about barking dogs. She was an okay dame.

She liked meddling in my cases, and I admit she helped solve a few. She claimed it wasn't that hard if you read *True Detective*. I don't know about that. I've read the *Sporting News* for years and can't thow a curveball. She liked using her brains and was a relentless researcher. She could assume any identity on the phone. She made a convincing cop, irate wife, or whatever role you asked her to play. Bette Davis had nothing on her.

I handled the typical private dick stuff: loose zippers, blackmail, stolen jewelry, inconvenient offspring, and all manner of misadventures. I was good at what I did. As my reputation grew, so did the status of my clients. There were always sticky situations people would rather the police not know about. Word-of-mouth is the best form of advertising in the sleuthing racket and discretion is coin-of-the-realm. When people with a few bucks needed a man who delivered and, more importantly, zipped his lips, that information passed from one well-heeled ear to the next over tea or cocktails. As my reputation grew, so did my fees. Catching rich wayward husbands was no harder than catching poor ones, but it sure as hell paid better. Lou Rizzo, P.I. had arrived.

"I asked you what you thought," reiterated Roz.

"About what?" I answered.

Her cheeks reddened and her jaw muscles tightened; they always did when I frustrated her, which I tried to do as often as possible. It was revenge for her assault on my drinking hobby.

"Hepburn's chance for an Oscar for *The African Queen*," she snapped. "What do you think I mean? What's your read on the murder of the century?"

"I'd say the killer had an issue with the groom."

"Brilliant," she deadpanned. "Do you think the killer acted alone."

"I don't know, but whoever pulled the trigger was a damn good shot."

I wasn't in the mood for a discussion, so I cut it off.

"Roz, Bill Newton is a good cop. He'll stumble around for a bit, but he'll get to the bottom of this. Until then, I have my own cases to worry about. I say let it be…which knowing you, you won't. While you're trying to solve the case from newspaper reports, let me remind you of *Rizzo's First Rule for Detecting: Whatever you think it is; it ain't.* Now, how about going back to your desk and doing whatever it is I'm paying you to do."

I can be an ass sometimes, especially when I'm grumpy or sober, which usually go together.

Chapter 3

Two days after the shooting, I was back in my office reading the latest *Globe* update on the case. The story dominated the headlines. Columns of newsprint were filled with rumor and speculation. Editorial pages demanded action. Today's lead story was, once again, under the byline of Dorothy Drake.

Chief investigator, Lt. William Newton summoned the press corps to his office to provide an update on the shocking murder at Riverfront Christian. He informed us that the organist, Abigail Clayborn, had recovered sufficiently from being rendered unconscious and was able to give a statement.

She testified that shortly after she had finished the Bridal Chorus, a man entered the choir loft. He had a press credential tucked in the band of his fedora. He carried a camera in one hand and an elongated canvas bag in the other which she assumed held a tripod. She motioned him to take off his hat since it was inappropriate in church. When he complied, she got a good look at him. He was approximately thirty years old, clean-shaven with a blonde crew cut. One distinguishing feature jumped out at her: He had a slight limp.

That was all she could tell the police because the next thing she remembers is waking up in the hospital. By its distinctive smell, doctors were able to verify that ether had been used to knock her out.

The coroner confirmed that the cause of death was a .30-06 slug that entered the victim's back, dissected his heart, and exited through the chest. A final report would be forthcoming.

Detective Newton provided one additional, tantalizing detail. A background check conducted on the victim had come up empty. No one in the financial world had ever heard of him. In fact, there was no evidence to suggest he ever existed. Detective Newton has asked anyone who has any information on Mr. Victor Jansen to come forward.

The Miller family declined to comment on their prospective son-in-law's mysterious past.

That was an interesting twist that added a layer of intrigue. When Roz figured I had enough time to read the article, she appeared in the doorway, a cup of coffee in one hand and a cigarette in the other. She wore a navy wool skirt and a matching navy blouse. A strand of fake pearls dangled from her neck. She wanted to talk. There was no getting around it this time without really aggravating her and that would drop the office temperature thirty degrees. I relented.

"Okay, pull up a chair, and let's hear your theory," I said.

She planted herself in one of the two client chairs opposite my desk, crossing her legs at the ankles.

"What do you think of the latest bombshell?" she asked.

"You first," I said.

"Okay. Let's start with the victim. He was either a gigolo or running a con. Victor Jansen's probably not his real name. The question is what was his game? Was he marrying into money and planning to live the high life or was there another angle?"

"Agreed. Jansen's a bogus name. As for his game, who knows. Could be anything," I said.

"Right, so let's look at motive."

"A rival suitor for Miss Miller's hand?" I offered.

"Not likely. She's twenty-eight, an old maid. Her best prospects had been snapped up long ago by more attractive rivals."

I'd seen her photo in the *Globe*. I thought she looked swell. Women can be pretty tough on other females. Ask a man and a woman to describe the same dame and nine-out-of-ten times, the woman will be more critical.

"Her looks," I said, "are immaterial. All that matters is that she's rich. Marry her and he'd be on easy street the rest of his life. He could afford all the extra dames he could handle."

"Men are disgusting."

"I was just stating the facts."

"So was I," she replied.

"How about revenge as a motive?" she said. "The groom's running a con and someone, maybe a partner, gets cut out of the deal when he decides to marry the mark. The killer decides to even the score by cutting Jansen out permanently."

"Why do it in such a public setting?" I asked.

"To add insult to injury."

"Hard to humiliate a stiff," I countered.

"Okay, try this one on for size. Maybe the groom had a jealous lover," she said.

"Again, why choose a public place? Where did she get an M-1? And who is this mysterious lover, Annie Oakley? That wasn't an easy shot. What's the distance from the choir loft to the altar? Fifty, maybe sixty yards? An M-1 is good up to 300 yards, so hitting a guy from that range is no great shakes. But drilling him right through the heart? That's good shooting."

"I guess you're right," she said. "Let me think about this a little more. See if I can come up with a better theory."

"Any chance you could do some thinking about one of our cases?"

"Speaking of our cases, you have a potential client coming in at 10 AM. A woman. Says she has a matter that must be handled discretely. I told her that's what we do. Couldn't get any more out of her. She said she wasn't in the habit of conducting business with the office staff and would only talk to the principal."

"That's not unusual."

"It wasn't what she said, it was the dismissive way she said it."

"You need a thick skin in this business."

"Mark my words, this one is going to be trouble. Having said her piece, she left.

I glanced at my watch...9:15. Efficient girl, that Roz.

Chapter 4

I opened the door to my office washroom and examined myself in the mirror. Medium height, medium build, brown eyes, and a patch over the left eye socket. I ran a comb through my dark hair, slicked back with Brylcream. I rubbed a hand across my chin and felt the stubble, even though my shave was only a few hours old. It was the dago curse, a permanent five o'clock shadow. I snugged-up my tie and checked it for stains. For a change, there weren't any. I pronounced myself fit to meet a new client, especially a dame.

The thing about the P.I. game is that you're never sure who will walk through the door or what they might want. Most of the time it's routine, but sometimes you're caught by surprise. I checked my watch, twenty minutes to go. I decided to contemplate the possibilities over a whiskey. I reached under the desk and extracted a flask from an old holster that I had nailed to the bottom of the drawer. It takes ingenuity to stay ahead of Roz. I unscrewed the top and took a swig. It was water.

There was a knock at the outer door, then the sound of high heels. Two muffled female voices conversed briefly, then I heard Roz say, "You're five minutes early. Mr. Rizzo is on the line with another client. He will see you at the appointed time. Please take a seat and make yourself comfortable."

She made her wait for ten, then the door to my office opened and Roz stuck her head in.

"A Miss Purcell to see you." She rolled her eyes which meant she didn't approve.

"Send her in."

A woman entered. She was easy on the eyes. I rose from my chair, stepped around the desk, and extended my hand. She grasped it, held on a beat longer than necessary, and made very direct eye-contact. It was strangely unnerving. She was a long drink of water. In heels, her green eyes were level with mine. Her red hair fell to her shoulders in waves. A simple violet dress highlighted alabaster skin. The dress was tailored to perfection, highlighting a figure that wouldn't quit. She wore a matching felt hat and carried a thin leather purse.

She checked me over, taking no apparent notice of my patch. It was a rare client indeed who didn't get around to commenting on it. I offered her a seat which she took, crossed her legs with a flourish, and adjusted the hem of her dress which fell just below her knees, providing an excellent view of a pair of shapely gams.

"Tell me, Miss Purcell, what brings you here today?"

"I have a matter that requires the utmost discretion."

"That's coin-of-the-realm around here."

"This will require more coin than usual," she said.

"Trust me."

She leaned forward and shot me a look that would have frozen the eyelashes off Lucifer's sister.

"Let's get something straight, Mr. Rizzo. I don't trust anyone."

"Then why are you here?"

"Because I need your help."

"Then why don't we stop this little waltz and get down to business. You need help. That means you need to trust somebody, and you're sitting in my office. Let's have it."

She leaned back in her chair, fished a silver cigarette holder from her purse, and flipped it open.

"Mind if I smoke?"

I shook my head and produced a lighter. She took a gloved hand and guided it to the tip of her smoke, maintaining eye contact the entire time. She took a deep drag and exhaled.

"I need your word that everything I tell you will remain between the two of us."

"I told you I was discreet."

"Whether you take the job or not?"

"That's in the Private Dick's Code. I've got it memorized."

"This is no time for a bad attempt at wit. Do I have your word or not?"

"I won't breathe a word."

"Fine. We have a deal. Mr. Rizzo..."

"Call me Lou...and we have no deal at the moment, other than my guarantee of confidentiality."

"Very well, Lou." She took another drag on her cigarette. "I want you to find the man who murdered my brother."

That caught me by surprise. I don't take murder cases. I did once and nearly got myself killed.

"I'm sorry, Miss Purcell, but murders are a police matter. Private eyes won't touch them. We can't afford to get crossways with the fuzz. Having a second party stomping around in one of their investigations can blow the whole thing apart in court. Have you gone to the police?"

"No."

"Why not?"

"I wouldn't do well in prison."

"You did something illegal?"

"Some small minds might think so."

"Do the police know your brother's dead?"

"Yes."

"Do they know he's been murdered?"

"Yes."

"Do they know about you?"

"No. That's enough of the third degree. Will you take the case or not?"

"I charge fifty bucks a day with a week payable in advance."

That was double my usual rate, but I wanted to scare her off. It didn't.

"We have a deal?" she asked.

No way I was taking the case, but I wasn't anxious to part company with the doll sitting across from me. I decided to make a play.

"It's a lot to swallow in one gulp. I need to think about it. Tell you what, I'll let you know over dinner. Pick you up at seven."

"Why would I go to dinner with you?" she said in a snobbish manner.

"Because you want me to do something illegal and I guess that you figure you can use your feminine charms to convince me to do it. You might be right. You'll never know unless you try."

"I haven't asked you to do anything illegal."

"Not yet, but you plan to."

Her crimson lips betrayed a hint of a smile. "How do you like my chances?"

"I'll tell you over a plate of *Linguine Alle Vongole* at *Pasquale's*. Where should I pick you up?"

"The lobby of the Mayfair."

"Are you staying there?"

"Quite the detective."

She stubbed out her cigarette, clutched her purse, and made her way out without a word...none was needed. Her exit made a statement of its own. I heard her footsteps as she passed Roz's desk and out the front door. No pleasantries were exchanged. As soon as it closed, Roz materialized in front of my desk.

"Do we have a new client?" she asked.

"As if you didn't know. I saw your shadow below the door which means your ear was up against it."

"I'm inquisitive by nature. That's why you keep me around."

"Yeah, I've often wondered why. Well, what do you think?"

"She's going to get you in trouble...big trouble."

"Woman's intuition?"

"I don't need any intuition; it's obvious. Anyone with two eyes can see it."

"I've only got one."

"Can the vaudeville routine. There's a reason we don't take cases like this. Cops don't give a damn about our stray zipper trade, but get in the way of a murder investigation and they'll grind you into sausage and serve you with eggs and toast. I know her type. She has a way with men...her way."

"We're just having dinner."

"Yeah, sure, and Lincoln was just going to the theatre."

Chapter 5

After Roz huffed back to her desk, I turned my attention to another case I was wrapping up. My client was a banker who had gotten himself in a pickle, or rather it was his pickle that had gotten him into trouble. He was being blackmailed by a woman who claimed to be the mother of his illegitimate son. She wanted five grand, or she would introduce his wife to the newest bastard in the family.

The heel had the dough but figured that even if he did pay, that wouldn't be the end of it. That brought him to me, Lou Rizzo, patron saint of the skirt-chaser. He wanted me to discredit the paternity claim and ensure his wife never got a whiff of his tomcatting. He gave me a week's advance to make his problem go away. My rate was twenty-five bucks a day. It only took four days, but I figured to milk the louse for another seventy-five. He had it coming. *Rizzo's First Rule of Professional Ethics: If the client hasn't any of his own, he's not entitled to any of yours.*

The SOB copped to hitting the sheets with the lady in question. She was a barmaid named Lucille who worked at a joint called *Tooley's*. I knew the place, but then I knew most of the watering holes in town. Years of research. I dropped by *Tooley's* for a quick one and a chat with the bartender who remembered me by my patch. I asked about Lucille. He told me she quit about six months ago without giving a reason, but he'd bet a bottle of his watered-down whiskey she had one in the oven. It took a few more drinks and a fin, but I got him to give me an address to a row-house in Hyde Park.

I paid a visit. A fat guy in a wife-beater and suspenders answered my knock. When I asked about the lady in the question, he said he was her husband, and she wasn't available. When I told him I was there to arrange for a payment, he changed his mind and ushered me in. He called for his wife who turned out to be a plain-looking broad carrying an infant on her hip. I got down to brass tacks, asking her if she could prove my client was the father. She claimed he had to be since her husband had a war injury and couldn't raise the flag. The fat guy seemed unaffected by his wife's candor and advised me that my client better pay them or be prepared to face the consequences.

The whole thing stunk. It was a shakedown and a bad one at that, but it didn't mean my client was out of the woods. Someone needed to put the fear of God into these two amateurs. Fortunately, I knew just the guy.

Picker is a mysterious character. No one knows his real name. He got the tag because he could pick anything...a pocket, a lock, or your bank account. He never got caught and never drew attention to himself because he never went for the big score. That would invite too much interest from the cops. He practiced his craft only as necessary to support his lifestyle which judging by his suits and expensive haircut was none too modest. He was tall dark and handsome, as the dames liked to say, and could charm the garters off a preacher's wife. Roz had a serious crush on him but so did every woman he met.

Once, I bailed him out of a tight spot when someone fitting his description was fingered as a burglary suspect. The cops were circulating a sketch that bore a striking resemblance. They were saturating his territory and applying the heat. He approached me in a bar and said he heard I was good and wanted me to find the real perp. Said he'd take care of the rest and not to worry, he wouldn't do anything illegal. Since I didn't know him, I wasn't sure I could trust him. I told him no. He said he'd double my fee. Turns out, I can be had.

He operated in the murky underbelly of society, so he had a few leads the police never would. Long story short, I found the guy and passed Picker the name. Two days later the perp strolled into his local station house and confessed. Picker can be quite convincing.

He said if I ever needed a favor to put the word on the street, and he'd show up. On several occasions, I had, including this one.

As he tells it, two nights after my visit with the blackmailers they returned from a stroll to find a nattily dressed visitor sitting on their threadbare couch. He was smoking a Cuban cigar, relaxed and unarmed. A brief conversation ensued during which the visitor calmly explained what the consequences would be if they foolishly pursued their plan. He asked them if they had any questions. They didn't. He had prepared a document for their signature admitting to the blackmail and denying any paternity claims against my client. He said they were eager to sign.

All that remained to be done was to let my client know he was off the hook and collect the rest of my fee. I was mulling over how soon I could sneak out of the office for a celebratory snort when I heard the phone ring in the outer office. Roz stuck her head in.

"Bill Newton's on the line."

Under normal circumstances that would have been welcome news, but I knew Newton was up to his eyeballs in the Victor Jansen murder. I wanted no part of that, but what could I do? He was a cop. I picked it up.

"Rizzo here."

"Lou, It's Bill Newton, you got time for a drink with an old friend?"

"Business or pleasure?"

"How about one for each, my treat."

No would have been the right answer, but a friend with the St. Louis Police Department was a handy arrow to have in your quiver.

"Well, if you're treating," I said, "I guess I could squeeze you in. Where and when?"

"Tonight, *The Warning Track*, 8 PM."

"Got a meeting with a client tonight, Can I get a raincheck for tomorrow?"

"Any other guy I'd figure for a hot date, but despite your swashbuckling good looks, I've never known you to have one. I guess I can survive another day without your company. See you tomorrow night."

Chapter 6

The Mayfair was an eighteen-story terra cotta and brick edifice on St. Charles St. not too far from my office on Walnut. I left my '51 Mercury with the valet, told him I'd be back in fifteen minutes, and entered the street-level lobby. It was nicely appointed with tile floors, dark wood paneling, and plenty of crystal chandeliers. A few guests were milling around but no stunning redheads. I looked at my watch, 6:50. Plenty of time for a drink.

I made my way to the bar and ordered a whiskey neat. The bartender pointed to my patch.

"Get that during the war?" he asked.

"Yup, a present from the emperor."

"Tough hand to be dealt," he commiserated.

"Could have been worse."

"I know. Lost two brothers. One on Utah beach and one on the *Indianapolis*. Me, I got a souvenir from a German .88 that I carry around. A little lower and to the right and I'd be a soprano."

I knew a little about .88s. It was an antiaircraft round but was occasionally used as an anti-armor weapon. It was a nasty piece of business.

"It never ends," I said. "Now the boys are slogging it out in Korea. For what? Old men place the bets, but young men pay the dealer. Always been that way. Always will."

The bartender poured himself a drink and refilled mine. He raised his glass in a toast.

"To young men everywhere. May God protect them."

"From what?" asked a feminine voice from behind me. She was wearing a white silk dress off one shoulder that was made for a dame like her. The other shoulder was ruffled and cut diagonally across the bodice, accentuating what lay beneath. It clung like a second skin and fell to mid-calf. The evening was cool; she carried a wrap. The bartender was gawking, his lower jaw slightly open.

"From what?" she repeated.

"I'm sorry. I don't get what you're asking?" I said.

"The toast. May God protect young men everywhere. Protect them from what?"

"From dames like you," I said, earning a smile.

I turned to the bartender. "What do I owe you?"

He waved me off. "On the house."

I touched two fingers above my right brow in a parting salute, then placed a hand gently on the lady's elbow and steered her towards the front door.

"You're pretty daring," I said.

"Why is that?"

"Wearing white to an Italian restaurant. You might need to wear a bib."

She glanced down at her décolletage, then back at me.

"I really don't think that's what you want me to do."

"I suppose not, but you'd better be careful."

"I'm always careful."

We stepped outside, and I signaled the valet for my car. The dark red Mercury arrived quickly. The kid left it running and sprang from the driver's seat. He double-timed past the chrome grill and opened the passenger side allowing the lady to flow in like smooth bourbon into a crystal tumbler. She favored him with a smile that buckled the kid's knees. I tipped him generously and got in the driver's side. I pulled the Merc into traffic and made my way west.

"We'll be dining on The Hill this evening. Do you know it?" I asked.

"I'm not from around here," she replied.

"Well then, you'll need a little geography lesson. The Hill is an Italian neighborhood off Route 100, just south of Forest Park. It got the moniker because it's near the highest point in the city. It's also known as Dago Hill. Yogi Berra and Joe Garagiola were raised there. You ever heard of them?"

"They're both good catchers, only Berra can hit," she said.

"A doll like you knows baseball?"

"My father was a big Indians fan. We'd sit around the breakfast table every morning pouring over box scores."

"You're from Ohio, then?"

"We moved around a lot."

That put a cork in that subject. I tried another.

"Since I'm taking you to dinner, it would be nice to know you're first name."

"What would you like it to be?"

"I'd settle for the truth."

"Do you think Anne suits me?"

"It's as good as anything."

"Then Anne it is."

It was a short drive to our destination on Hereford Street. Pasquale's was a converted brick storefront. There was a space directly in front and I maneuvered the Merc in. I escorted Anne through the front door where we were met by the owner's son Gianni Savino.

"Ah, Signore Rizzo. It is so good to see you. Will you and *la signora* be joining us this evening? But of course, you will. Would you like your regular table or one more suitable for two?"

Chapter 7

Gianni led us to one of a dozen tables that occupied the small dining room. Like all the others, it had a red and white checked tablecloth lit by a candle stuck in a straw-wrapped chianti bottle. Waves of dried wax spilled down the side. The table setting identified it as a working-class joint. The high-class places had white tablecloths and crystal lamps. I stumbled across Pasquale's a few years back and tried to hit it once a month. The food was great, and they treated me like family.

A busboy materialized with water, fresh bread, and a saucer sprinkled with olive oil and oregano. That was followed by a waiter with a bottle of chianti.

"Compliments of Mr. Savino," he said while pouring us both a glass.

I glanced over at Gianni and he smiled back at me.

"They seem to know you around here," said Anne.

"It's my little secret."

"Does that explain while you usually dine alone?"

"I dine alone for obvious reasons. Most women aren't interested in damaged goods."

She leaned back and took a sip of wine while she considered me.

"Well, I think you're handsome...in a primitive way."

Not so primitive that I didn't recognize when I was being worked.

"I bet you say that to all the boys."

"Believe what you will."

She picked up her menu, thought about it, then placed it back down.

"What did you say you were going to order for us?"

"*Linguine Alle Vongole*...linguine with clams, but with a twist. It's usually served with an olive oil and white wine sauce. Gianni uses a Sangiovese, crushed San Marzano tomatoes, paste, and dried Calabrian chiles. Gives it a gentle kick. Best in town. Gianni uses littlenecks. Brings them up from the gulf. You game?"

"How can I refuse?"

The meal was delicious, and the staff fawned over us. I tried to pump her for personal information, leaving the professional ones for later. I like to know who I'm dealing with. Most people enjoyed nothing better than talking about themselves, but she was evasive. Our conversation was a verbal fencing match, every thrust deftly parried.

I was more forthcoming. She found out I was raised in Jersey, the only son of Italian immigrants. My dad drove a truck, and my mom took in washing to make ends meet. As a kid, I developed a fascination with airplanes and spent every spare nickel I earned on *Popular Mechanics*. Every issue had at least one aviation article. I cut out the best photos and hung them on the walls until my room became a museum. After high school, I tried college, but the classroom didn't suit me. In 1939 I enlisted in the Army and parlayed my two semesters of college into an aviation cadet slot. I was commissioned and got my wings at Randolph Field in San Antonio. As far as I was concerned, life was as good as it got. My plan was to serve-out my military commitment, then make a career flying for an airline. But then came the war, the loss of an eye in combat, and there went my dream.

Anne listened intently without interrupting, like a tigress lying silent in the tall grass, observing her prey.

When we finished, our waiter cleared the table and brought us two steaming demitasse cups filled with a dark, robust coffee. Anne started to add a lump of sugar to hers, but I motioned her to wait. I asked the waiter to bring us two shots of anisette.

"Pour it in your coffee," I said, "then take a sip. My parents drank it this way. Tell me what you think."

She brought the cup to her lips and sampled the contents.

"It's very nice," she purred. "so was dinner, and I don't believe I spilled any sauce. Care to inspect me?"

"Gravy," I said.

She gave me a quizzical look.

"What?"

"Jersey dagoes call it gravy."

"But It's a sauce."

"Tell that to my mom. If it's white, you can call it a sauce; if it's red, it's gravy."

She switched lanes. "Time to talk business. Will you take the case or not?"

"I'm still debating. I need to ask a few questions first. You haven't answered any so far. Are you game?"

"Up to a point."

"For starters, what was your brother's name?"

"Richard, but he went by "Victor Jansen.""

That was one hell of a gut-shot. I almost choked on my coffee. To paraphrase Bogart's Ric Blaine in *Casablanca: Of all the stiffs in all the world why'd she have to drop this one in my lap?*

"The guy gunned down at the altar? Are you crazy? Every flat-foot within a hundred-mile radius is working that case. The heat from the top is so intense the cops have to stick their heads in the oven to cool off. They're going to find the guy. You don't need me."

"I need you to find him first, and I can give you information the police don't have. You'll have a head start."

"Why do I need to find him before the cops?"

"Because I intend to kill him."

My first thought was she was kidding; my second she was crazy; my third was I needed to head for the exit.

"Look, doll. There's not enough scratch in the world to make me an accessory to murder."

"But, no one will know you were involved."

"You will."

"I couldn't betray you without betraying myself," she said.

"Yes, you could. If things go wrong, you might try pinning the whole thing on me. By the way, why bother to kill a guy when the state will be happy to give him an electric send-off?"

"I have my reasons."

"I'm sorry, but I can't help you."

"I'll make it worth your while."

"I don't need the money that badly."

She reached under the table and rested a hand gently on my knee. The candlelight highlighted the gold specks in her eyes. Those babies were dangerous. She dropped her voice to a throaty whisper and leaned in.

"Who said anything about money?"

She must have taken me for a fool. It was perceptive of her. I took the case. Too many dinners alone, I guess.

We finished our coffee and headed back to the Mayfair. She didn't say much, allowing me time to consider what I planned to do. There was something off about this caper, and I needed time to work it out. I'd slow walk the investigation and give the cops a wide berth. That would also give me extra time to spend with the mysterious Miss Purcell.

The valet, desk clerk, and bartender were still on duty as we made our way through the lobby to the elevator. Any of them would have gladly changed places with me. Later, in her room, she offered me a nightcap, double whiskey neat, and laid-out the details of the scam she and her brother were running. I asked a few questions, and she answered. Then she made a down payment on future services rendered.

Chapter 8

The following morning, I managed to stop by my house for a shower, shave, and change of clothes before heading to the office. It didn't do much good. Roz was waiting to greet me.

"You took the case, didn't you?"

"What makes you say that?"

"You still have a rancid whiff of redhead about you."

I was dead on my feet, and my head pounded like a jackhammer.

"Let me get some coffee before you start the inquisition. Got any aspirin?"

I went to my office and examined myself in the washroom mirror. The man who stared back at me with one bloodshot eye looked like a guy who'd been through the wringer. I grabbed my mug and went back to the outer office. Roz flipped me an aspirin bottle. I poured a fistful of the little white tablets and downed them with black coffee.

"Tie one on last night?" asked Roz.

"You'd have been proud of me, only two glasses of chianti and a nightcap."

"That makes it worse. I expect you to do dumb things when you're drunk, you got into this mess sober."

"It's an interesting case."

"It's a murder case," she protested, but I knew her curiosity would get the best of her.

I decided on the way to the office to give her the straight dope. For her protection, I planned to leave out the part about our client's murderous intent.

"Do you want to know the details or not?"

"All right, let's have them."

"Anne, that's her name, and her brother, Richard, are a confidence team."

"What's so interesting about that?"

"For their current swindle, Richard was using the handle Victor Jansen."

"Whoa there, boss," interrupted Roz, her eyes wide as saucers. "The dead groom?"

"One and the same. They were running a scam on Mercedes Miller who they met at a cocktail party in Havana."

"Whom."

"What?" I asked.

"It's 'whom' they met."

"Damn your liberal arts education."

"It's a curse," she said. "Why Havana?"

"Same reason fishermen go where the fish are. It's a playground for the rich. They'd been running a variation on this grift for years and had it perfected. Once the victim was identified, they went to work. Richard would arrange to meet, seduce, and propose to a lonely little rich girl while Anne made sure that the background story they concocted would hold up under scrutiny by the mark's family.

"As the wedding grew closer, Richard would approach the bride's father and confess he was a con artist and had sullied his daughter. For a fee, in this case fifty grand, he would disappear, providing a cover story guaranteed to ensure the lady's virtue. The fact that it would break the bride's heart was unfortunate but unavoidable. If the father balked, Richard would threaten to disappear anyway, but not before leaking the details to the press and ruining the girl's reputation for life.

"Something went wrong this time. Richard fell in love and decided to go through with the wedding. Anne was not happy about losing her share of the payoff, but her brother assured her that he'd take care of her. She could have exposed him, but there was nothing to be gained doing that, so she eventually resigned herself to the situation. Then, someone killed him. That's the story. What do you think?"

"I'm going to need a minute to think this through."

She rose from her desk, poured herself another cup of coffee, and took a few sips.

"This whole thing doesn't sound right. She said she had her reasons for wanting to find the guy before the cops. Why?"

"She didn't say," I lied.

"Is she trying to protect herself?"

"From what?"

"If somebody got wise to the shakedown, perhaps that same somebody knew about her role and could reveal it to the cops."

"What could she do about that?" I asked.

"She'd have to kill him," she replied.

She had gotten to the truth in a hurry. So much for not implicating her. "You think your redheaded squeeze has got the moxie?"

"She's not my squeeze."

"Of course not, you're being played. If she's going to kill him, we're going to be accessaries. I don't look good in stripes. They make me look well-fed. You need to tell her you've changed your mind."

"What if she just wants to avenge her brother's death?"

"It still means murder. The motive doesn't mean a thing. Listen to what you're saying."

I don't think I ever disliked Roz more than when she was right, and that was way too often.

"You're probably right. I'm gonna be useless today. Let me go home and sleep on it," I said.

"That better be all you're sleeping on."

"I'll be thinking more clearly tomorrow. I need some rest."

"Fine, but don't forget you have dinner tonight with Bill Newton. What are you going to tell him?"

It was a damn good question.

Chapter 9

The Warning Track was a bar on Sullivan St. in the shadow of Sportsman Park, home to both the Browns of the American League and the Cardinals of the National League. It was a non-descript joint, well off the beaten path, a good place to knock a few back out of the public eye. It was a favorite hangout for cops.

It was raining when I parked the Merc on an adjacent side street. I raised the collar of my trench coat and secured my fedora. I sloshed through the puddles to the front door. Once inside, I took off my coat and hat and shook myself dry like a wet dog. A few heads turned. I was a familiar figure to the law and hard to miss with my patch. There was a smattering of hellos as I scanned the room. Bill was in a corner booth lit by a low-watt bulb under a green shade. He was working on a beer, probably not his first. I slid into the bench seat opposite him. He looked like he hadn't slept in a week

"Hey, Bill," I said. "How's it going?"

The tall man, twenty years my senior with a receding hairline and spare tire, paused to consider the question. He offered me a wry smile.

"If you read the papers, you wouldn't have to ask."

"Not so well?"

"The worst. The Captain, the Chief, the Commissioner, and the Mayor are on my ass to solve this case, and I'm not making much progress. I thought maybe a new set of eyeballs, or in your case, eyeball might help."

"What about all these other cops in here? Are they avoiding you?"

"They're okay, they're following the primary survival rule in any bureaucracy."

"Which is?"

"If the boat is sinking, don't grab the anchor. I'm the biggest anchor in the fleet. You're not a part of the system, so what do you say. Will you hear me out?"

"Depends. You gonna buy me a drink or not?"

"I'll throw in dinner."

He waved a waitress over and ordered a couple of beers. We also ordered the dinner special, sausages over fried potatoes, grilled onions, and smothered in brown gravy. She took our order and returned with our drinks.

"You must eat here often," I said gesturing to his belly.

"The wife says I'm bad company when working a tough case. Says the less she sees of me, the better it is for all concerned. At least she lets me sleep in my own bed."

"Mighty generous of her."

"Yup, she's a regular peach."

"All right, Bill. What have you got?"

"I take it you have the basics. This Victor Jansen guy gets plugged at his wedding by a shot from the choir loft. Seventy yards, right through the ticker. Damn fine shooting especially with an M-1. The first cop up the stairs saw the organist, a Mrs. Clayborn, out like a light on the floor. He also found the rifle on the first stairwell landing. A liquid-soaked handkerchief, an empty bottle, a long canvas bag, and a pair of binoculars were also found on the floor. The Clayborn dame is the only one who saw the assailant.

"She was hauled off to City Hospital. When she came to, she described a man who she said was a photographer. He carried a camera and a canvas bag that she assumed held a tripod. She said he was about six feet with a blond crewcut and a long, thin face. Said he walked with a slight limp. He wore a press pass tucked in the band of his fedora. Clayborn turned back to the organ to prepare for the first hymn, *Abide*

With Me. That's when someone grabbed her from behind and covered her mouth and nose. She remembers a sweet smell. That's the last she remembered before the world went black. The handkerchief smelled like ether as did the small pharmacy bottle we found next to it."

"Any prints on the rifle or the bottle?" I asked.

"Nothing."

"How about on the stairwell banister?"

"Hundreds which is the same as nothing."

"A pro?"

"Looks that way."

"Anything unusual about the crime scene?"

"The binoculars."

"Yeah, that is an odd twist, but it has to fit in the puzzle somewhere. Any chance they belonged to the organist?"

"Never saw them before in her life."

Dinner arrived. Newton ordered another beer. I waved off a refill. Roz would be proud. Dinner was typical tavern fare. There was enough grease left on the plate to lube the Merc.

We didn't discuss the case while we ate, bad for digestion. When we were through, the waitress cleared the table, Bill ordered a third beer...or was it his fourth? It was time to get back to business.

"Any leads on the photographer?" I asked.

"Better than that. We brought the guy in. Works as a stringer."

"Didn't read anything about that," I said.

"We're keeping it under wraps."

"I thought you said you weren't making progress."

"We're not. We gave the guy the bare lightbulb treatment, but he denied everything. We can place him at the church, but not the loft. He's got no record and no connection with the victim or the weapon. We're still digging but we're not gonna be able to keep him on ice much longer."

"Did he have a camera with him? The film might place his location at the time of the shooting. Maybe exonerate him."

"We thought of that, but he claims it was knocked out of his hand in the melee. He managed to retrieve it, but it had sprung open, and the film was exposed. Useless."

"What about the victim? Got a line on him yet?"

"It's like the guy never existed, but somehow he convinced one of the most prominent families in the city, not to mention the lady, that he was marriage material."

It was the perfect time to tell Bill about Jansen and his sister, but I passed.

"Didn't the family check him out?"

"They thought they did. Used some upscale dick name of Teller. References all checked, but Teller has been unable to locate any of them since."

"I've met this Teller guy once," I said. "A snappy dresser, fancies himself a sophisticate. He preys on the upper classes. Haven't heard a good word about him."

"All shine, no substance," offered Newton.

"Sounds like Jansen was running a scam," I said. "Maybe someone got wise and decided he needed to go away, permanent-like. Gotta be a less conspicuous way to do it, though."

"That's the wall I keep bumping into," said Bill. "Got any suggestions or even a theory?"

I liked Bill and hated being dishonest with him. My only play was to plead ignorance. I hoped to put him off.

"I don't have enough information. I'd have to see the whole file."

"I thought you might say that," he said reaching for a folder on the seat next to him. He slid it across to me. "Here's the whole mess. Enjoy."

That's the last thing I wanted. I was being sucked into the storm with no way out.

"This isn't by the book. You're sticking your neck out."

"Lou, it's already on the guillotine, and they're selling tickets for the privilege of dropping the blade."

Chapter 10

Roz beat me to the office the next morning. That made one hundred and sixty days in a row she could make that claim. She had the coffee pot going and Nat King Cole was crooning *Too Young* on the radio providing a mellow background that stood in stark contrast to the storm raging in my gut. I didn't like the way this game was playing out. I owed Bill Newton my loyalty. I didn't owe Anne Purcell a thing, but she had set the hook pretty good.

"How'd dinner with Newton go?" asked Roz.

"I didn't exactly lie, but I wasn't completely truthful with him either."

"Did you tell him Jansen was a con man?"

"He already suspected as much."

"Did you tell him his real name was Purcell and that his sister was your client?"

"No, but I agreed to help."

"That was big of you."

"He gave me this," I said tossing Newton's folder on her desk. "It's the Jansen file."

"The whole thing?"

"Yup."

"He must be desperate."

"Every brass-buttoned bureaucrat in town is breathing down his neck."

"Anything interesting in there?" she asked.

"I looked at the crime scene photographs. That's where you come in. I need you to filter through this stuff and see if there's something the cops missed. I'll understand if you don't want to get involved."

She picked up the folder and examined it. It was like catnip to her.

"I'm already involved. Can you give me a summary, so I know what I'm looking for?"

I repeated what Bill told me. Roz listened without interruption. When I was through, she said, "The binoculars are a strange detail."

I suggested we look at the crime scene photographs and compare observations. There were six. The first was a shot of the victim lying face down with a neat hole in the back of his white tuxedo jacket. No doubt the exit wound was messier. A puddle of blood had collected beneath him.

"I don't see anything useful here. You?"

"No clues I can see," said Roz.

The second photo was a shot of the choir loft from the altar. A uniform was standing in the middle, along the rail to provide perspective. The third was the reverse view, shot from the loft with three uniforms standing in for the bride, groom, and minister.

"Did Newton say anything about the bridal party?" asked Roz.

"No, but I'm sure they gave statements. That's probably worth looking into."

She nodded and took a note.

"I'm no marksman; that looks like a long way. How good would the shooter have to be?"

"Better than the average Joe."

The fourth photo was a shot of the abandoned murder weapon on the landing of the loft's staircase.

"How'd it end up there?" asked Roz.

"The killer probably tossed it there on his way out. Carrying a camera and a press pass is a lot less suspicious than an M-1."

"Why not just leave it in the loft?"

"Maybe he initially kept it as insurance in case he had to shoot his way out but thought better of it when he realized he could make his escape in the chaos. Then he just dropped it."

The fifth photo showed a taped outline of where the organist had been found. Visible near the head was a handkerchief. Also visible was a small bottle and beside that a cork.

The final photo was like the previous one but shot from further back giving a wider perspective. It captured the organist's bench about six feet from the body. A purse and hat were perched on it. It also captured a long canvas bag and binoculars near the loft rail.

"Got any theories on what the field glasses are all about?" asked Roz.

"Can't be to identify the groom. That would be obvious even from the loft. I'd guess the shooter was a hired gun. He was waiting for a signal from his employer to pull the trigger. The signal would have to be subtle. Maybe he needed the binoculars to pick it up."

"That would mean the guy who hired the shooter had to be family or a guest."

"Or a member of the bridal party," I added.

"We've got some work to do," she said.

"We? I thought you were opposed to us getting involved. Why the change of heart? What about my moral dilemma?"

"The Newton situation is your problem; you still need to come clean with him. That's not negotiable, but you're too busy skirt-chasing some third-rate *femme fatale* to see it. You know that. You also know that the chance to work on a case like this is too delicious for me to pass on. So, I'm going to rationalize my unethical behavior. I learned how from you."

"Our working theory," I said, ignoring the insult, "is the killer gained access to the loft disguised as a photographer, drugged the organist, and plugged the groom. What we don't know is who he was working for and what was the motive. Start digging through the file and see what you can find."

I stood up and grabbed my fedora from the tree rack by the entrance. "No one can pull off a caper like this without word leaking out to the street. I'm going to hit some of the usual spots and let it be known that I'm looking for Picker, then I'm going to pay a visit to a colleague. If Picker shows up while I'm gone, keep him entertained.

"With pleasure," she said, and I knew she meant it.

Chapter 11

The five-story office building occupied a corner lot in a prosperous-looking professional district. I entered the lobby and looked at the registry. The offices of Archer L. Teller, Private Investigator were located on the top floor. I summoned the elevator and rode the car up. The doors opened to a well-appointed waiting room presided over by a severe-looking, middle-aged woman with salt-and-pepper hair pulled back tightly and fastened near the nape of her neck with a clip. She eyed me warily as I approached.

"May I help you, sir?"

"Yes, as a matter of fact, you may. I'd like to see Mr. Teller. Is he in?"

"Do you have an appointment?"

She had his appointment book on her desk, so I imagined she knew I didn't. I decided it would be impolite to point that out. Instead, I mustered my most winning smile. Gatekeepers are all the same. They are best approached cautiously and on bended knee.

"I'm afraid I don't. I was hoping Mr. Teller might be able to spare me a few moments. I am sure he leaves the details of his schedule in your capable hands. Do you think you might be able to squeeze me in?"

She made a show of thumbing through some papers.

"Let me see if he's available. Who may I say is calling?"

"Rizzo, Louis Rizzo."

"And your business?"

"A matter of mutual interest."

She raised an eyebrow and shrugged. She threw a switch on the intercom. A tinny voice came over the speaker.

"Yes, Mrs. Lord?"

"A gentleman is here to see you. Mr. Louis Rizzo. Says he wants to discuss a matter of mutual interest."

After a brief pause, the voice came back.

"Very well, show him in."

She rose from her desk and motioned me to follow her to an oak door. It had a brass plate engraved with the name Archer L. Teller. She knocked once, opened it, announced me, and retreated, closing the door behind her.

An aristocratic-looking gentleman in an expensive wool pinstripe rose from behind his desk and extended his hand. He stood over six feet tall and had a lean build. His gray hair sported an expensive cut. Ice-blue eyes betrayed his disapproval, despite the perfect smile.

"Archer Teller. You said we had some mutual interest?"

"Lou Rizzo," I replied. "I'm a P.I. also, and I'm working a case in which you may have some interest."

"I doubt that," he said. "My clients are rather high end. I suspect yours are not."

"My client," I said, "has an interest in the Victor Jansen case."

He stiffened.

"That's a police matter, Mr. Rizzo. I don't know what kind of agency you run, but even a neophyte knows better than to get involved."

"Why don't you let me worry about that," I said.

"I'll report you to the authorities."

"Fine, that will give me chance to tell them how you botched a simple background check. That might be professionally embarrassing. Can't imagine that would be good for business. Might have to move to a more modest location. Maybe even let Mrs. Lord go. I bet she looks a lot different with her hair down."

It was a shot-in-the-dark, but it landed. Teller's controlled demeanor fell away.

"Be careful, Rizzo," he snarled. "I have the resources to make life difficult for you. Maybe impossible."

"Come on, Teller. Sweet talking will get you nowhere. Let's stop sparring and discuss business."

He regained his composure and went back to his desk.

"Very well, pull up a chair. Care for a drink?"

"A whiskey would be nice."

He pushed the intercom. "Sarah, would you be so kind as to fetch us a couple of whiskeys and bring your note pad."

We sat in silence assessing each other until the drinks arrived. Sarah took a chair out of my line of sight.

"Okay, Mr. Rizzo who is your client, and what do they want you to do?"

"Well, Archie…"

"It's Archer if you please," he said making no effort to conceal his irritation.

Good. I wanted to get the pompous ass off his game.

"That, as you know, Archie is confidential. But I can tell you this; they know that Victor Jansen was a confidence man. They believe if the wrong people found out about the scam, it might have led to his murder."

"Go on," he said.

"They believe there are several possible suspects. One of whom is you. What do you say to that?"

His jaw muscles tightened, his face turned red and the veins popped on his neck. He stood up and pounded his desk with both fists.

"This is preposterous. I warned you to watch your tongue. Get out of my office. You made a very grave mistake. There will be appropriate consequences."

I rose and downed the rest of my drink. It was the good stuff and I wasn't about to waste it."

"Does this mean," I asked, "that we won't be collaborating on the case?"

"Get the hell out of here right now," he bellowed.

"Good day, Archie," I said. I'll show myself out."
Rizzo's First Rule of Investigative Chaos. When the pot's cold, start a fire.

I'd know soon enough if Teller had something to hide.

Chapter 12

It was late afternoon when I made it back to the office. Roz had the contents of the Jansen folder organized in three stacks on her desk. She'd been busy.

"The prodigal son returns," she chided. "Who was the mysterious colleague you bolted out of here to see?"

"The one-and-only Archer L. Teller, society sleuth."

"Do tell. How'd that go?"

"We may have gotten off on the wrong foot."

"What did you hope to accomplish?"

"I didn't have any idea, but I knew if we were going to get this baby rolling, I needed to kick the hornets' nest."

"What did you tell him?"

"That I considered him a suspect."

"And he took offense to a little thing like that?"

"Thought he'd blow a gasket."

"How'd you set it up?"

"I told him we had a client who had an interest in the case, and we were conducting an independent investigation. He threatened to report me to the police, but he lost his steam when I told him I'd make his shoddy work for the Millers public knowledge."

"Shot him in the wallet," she grinned.

"How about you? Did you get anything useful out of the police file?"

"Pull up a chair, and I'll give you the dope. There was a lot of stuff to wade through. Some of it was a bureaucratic waste of paper, that's the first stack," she said pointing to the largest pile. "Then there are the witness statements and detective work; that's the second stack. Finally, there are the photos. Where do you want to start?"

I grabbed a chair and lit a cigarette.

"Let's have a look at those pictures one more time."

She slid the photo of the victim toward me. He was still a stiff.

"The paper said the bride's father escorted her off the altar. Does that check with the witness accounts?" I asked.

"Yes, it does," answered Roz.

"Did anyone try to assist the victim?"

"Nothing in the file about that."

"That's odd. You'd think someone would have rolled him over to see if he could be helped. What about the preacher?"

"He went with the bride and her father."

"The best man? The groomsmen?"

"Nothing in the files indicating they tried to help."

"Fine bunch of friends they turned out to be."

"They weren't his friends. The best man was the bride's brother, the groomsmen her cousins. According to the Miller family, Jansen was an orphan."

"An orphan is one thing, but a man with no friends is harder to explain," I said.

"Doesn't seem like anyone bothered to ask," said Roz, "it's not in the file."

"What about the maid-of-honor and bridesmaids?"

"The maid-of-honor was a childhood friend; the bridesmaids were cousins."

"What's the brother's name?"

"Patrick P. Miller, Jr."

"Did he have a bone to pick with the victim?"

"According to police interviews with family friends," she said touching the second stack, "he was in line to become the company president when his old man retired. The problem was that Senior thought Junior was too immature to handle the job. It was likely he would have handed control of the company to his new son-in-law."

"Do the police consider him a suspect?"

She rifled through the middle stack. "Yes, I've got a list of possible suspects here."

She handed me an official-looking document over Bill Newton's signature. It listed each of the possible suspects in priority order with a potential motive: The photographer (motive unknown), Patrick Miller Sr. (protect family name), Patrick Miller Jr. (financial interests), victim's accomplice (avenge double-cross), possible rejected suitor (lost opportunity to marry heiress).

"What do you think?" I asked her.

"Based on what you've told me, we need to add Teller. I still think Junior is the most obvious, but in the movies, it's never the obvious guy, is it?"

"If this were the movies, you'd be Lauren Bacall, doll."

"And you'd be Bogie, but without the sex appeal."

"Let's get back to the case. I think we can eliminate the unknown accomplice. Anne never mentioned one."

"Did you ask her?"

"Not directly, but she didn't hint at it and, if one existed and she suspected him, she wouldn't need our services. Let's see the other photos again."

She grabbed the last stack. The two perspective shots didn't reveal much, other than the loft rail would make a fine pedestal for the barrel of a rifle. The shot of the M-1 in the stairwell revealed nothing. The final two photos showing the placement of the organist's body and the other paraphernalia gnawed at me. I was sure the outline, handkerchief, bottle, canvas bag, and binoculars held a secret.

"There's a clue here. I know it, but I'll be damned if I can figure out what it is."

"Everything fits the narrative," said Roz.

"Maybe that's what bothers me."

Our conversation was interrupted by the telephone. Roz picked up.

"Lou Rizzo's office."

"Hello, Bill. Yes, he's here. Please hold."

I wondered how long it would take before my episode with Teller resulted in a call from Newton. I looked at my watch…two hours. Someone was generating major heat. Bill was in no mood to talk. His message was abrupt.

"Meet me at the usual place at eight sharp. And try not to step on any more toes between now and then."

He wasn't referring to the *Warning Track* but rather the docks opposite the federal courthouse. We'd meet there when he didn't want other cops to see us. The line went dead before I could respond.

I hadn't eaten all day and had two hours to kill before meeting Bill. I don't like having my butt chewed on an empty stomach. I looked at Roz.

"Can I buy you a coffee and sandwich at *Nestor's*? We can kick around a few ideas before I have to meet with Bill."

"Let the record show the condemned man ate a last meal," she quipped. "I could use a bite. Let's go."

Chapter 13

Nestor's was a diner around the corner from my office. It was the outer boundary of my social interaction with Roz. As always, we sat at the far end of the counter away from other customers; tonight, there weren't any. The guy who ran the place, Abe Berkowitz made the best Reuben in town, thick slices of corned beef, a hearty slab of swiss cheese, sauerkraut, and Russian dressing on dark Russian rye. We both ordered one. I lowered my voice to a whisper and leaned in.

"Abe, the lady would like a beer with her sandwich. Could you bring her one?"

"You know I don't sell booze, no liquor license."

"You mean you can't sell me a bottle?"

"That would be a violation, no? The city will shut me down."

"You misunderstand me. I don't want to buy one, but I wouldn't turn down a gift. No law against that, is there?"

It was his turn to switch to a whisper.

"You see any beer around here?"

"No, but if you go into the kitchen and crack open that old Frigidaire, I bet you can find a bottle."

I slid a fiver across the counter…about five times the going rate. It disappeared into his apron before you could say Jack Robinson.

"Let me check for you," he smiled.

"While you're at it, bring two. Bad manners to let a lady drink alone." I glanced at Roz, who shrugged.

"It's after office hours. One can't hurt," she said.

The sandwiches were served with fries, coleslaw, and a dill pickle. We went at them with a vengeance. I didn't say much, which wasn't unusual. Roz said nothing, which was front-page, top-of-the fold stuff. After a while, I began to worry about her. She finished her meal and pushed her plate away.

"Want to talk about the case?" I asked but got no response. "What's eating you?"

She wiped the grease from her mouth. It came with the territory where a Rueben is concerned. No way to eat one without getting a coating on your kisser. When she was done, she placed the napkin on the counter and looked directly into my eye.

"Lou, do you have a conscience?"

"Where the hell did that come from? What do you think?"

"To tell the truth, I'm not sure anymore. What you're doing to Bill Newton isn't right."

I started to speak, but she cut me off. The excited fledgling investigator from an hour ago had disappeared and been replaced by a brooding pile of suppressed fury. It happened right before my eyes, but I was too involved with my corned beef to notice. As usual, when it came to women, I had missed all the clues.

"His career is on the line, and you're using him to work a case for some manipulating ginger, a confessed criminal to boot. You might end up committing another crime before she's through with you."

"Another? I haven't committed one yet."

"You're withholding evidence. Last time I checked, that was a crime."

"What about my obligation to my client."

"You created that problem. She shouldn't be your client in the first place. Taking the case was foolhardy. I worry about what goes on above your collar and below your belt."

"If Bill gives me the opportunity tonight, I'll come clean."

"You need to come clean no matter what."

"I can't promise that."

"Fine," she said. It was the kind of *fine* a dame uses when you've lost the argument. As if on cue, she stood up, drained her beer, fished some bills out of her purse, and tossed them on the counter.

"Here's my share of the bill."

"Pick it up, Roz. It's my treat."

"I'll pay my own way, thank you. I won't need a lift home either. I can walk."

I looked out the front window. It was dark and a steady rain had begun to fall, splattering the glass with large liquid drops. A flash of lightning momentarily lit up the abandoned street. It was about five blocks to her walk-up. Hoofing it wasn't the smartest move on a nice night; it was crazy on one like this.

"C'mon, Roz. Let me give you a lift. It's miserable out there."

She grabbed her overcoat, put it on, flipped up the collar, and started for the door. Pivoting back, she snatched my fedora from the seat next to mine. Putting it on her head and pulling it down over her ears, she looked like she was mugging for a Martin and Lewis comedy. She left without a word.

Abe watched the drama from behind the counter.

"You can always tell when you've made a woman angry," he said. "She leaves without finishing her dinner." He grabbed the pickle off her plate and took a bite.

Chapter 14

I needed to get going to make my rendezvous with Bill. I flipped up the collar on my trench coat and headed for the door. The Merc was parked by the curb, but without my fedora, I was still going to get soaked. Abe came to the rescue with a wool snap-brim some drunk left a few weeks ago. It had seen better days, but beggars can't be choosers. I put it on and examined myself in an aluminum napkin holder. It was a bad look for a private eye. You would never catch Bob Mitchum in one of these babies.

I waved goodbye to Abe, sprinted to the driver's door, opened it, and got in behind the wheel. I took off the hat, tossed it on the passenger side, turned on the ignition and pulled out into the street. I thought briefly of catching up with Roz and giving her a lift the rest of the way but figured it would just make things worse. She was, no doubt, already soaked and in a foul mood. I headed for the dock.

What would normally have been a ten-minute drive stretched to twenty due to the downpour. Visibility was poor, and the streets were slick. As we used to say in the Army Air Corps, it was so miserable, even the ducks were grounded. The Merc's wipers thumped back-and-forth in a futile attempt to keep up with the deluge. When I reached the docks, I pulled up in front of the rendezvous point; an abandoned, rusting, corrugated steel warehouse which now housed only bums and an occasional floating poker game. My Merc was the only car there. I checked my watch. It was the appointed time. Bill was probably running late because of the weather.

Ten minutes passed, and the storm slacked off a bit. I saw a pair of headlights approaching from behind. When they got closer, I recognized the vehicle as the make and model cops used for unmarked cruisers. It pulled up alongside, and the driver rolled down his window. It was Bill Newton. I leaned across the front seat and cranked down the passenger window.

"Get your tail over here, Rizzo. We need a skull session; as in I'm going to crack yours."

He didn't leave much room for discussion. I rolled up the window and put on my hat which had added the smell of wet dog to its nasal arsenal. I ran around the front of the Merc and then to the cruiser. As soon as I opened the passenger door and jumped in, Bill gave me the once-over and wrinkled his nostrils.

"What the hell is that smell?"

"My new hat. You like it?"

"It looks like crap and smells worse."

"It's the latest fashion."

"Enough. What the hell were you thinking, ruffling Teller's feathers? You had to figure he was connected and would get his patrons to come down on the investigation. That means coming down on me. I'm getting to be on a first-name basis with the mayor."

"I thought we needed to get the ball rolling, and he was a good place to start. Did you know he's sleeping with his secretary?"

"Nope, don't give a damn either. He can shack-up with Eleanor Roosevelt for all I care. Got nothing to do with the case. What did you do to set him off?"

"I suggested he might be a suspect in the Jansen murder. He didn't take it too well."

"What? We don't have him as a suspect."

"Maybe you should. Think about it. He makes a living doing cushy work for well-heeled clients. If word gets out that he did a sloppy job on Jansen's background check, he stands to lose a lot of business. Suppose Jansen had attempted to shakedown the bride's family. The father goes to Teller and reads him the riot act; threatens to ruin him. Teller makes excuses and tells the old man not to worry; he'll fix the problem. By the way, was Teller a wedding guest?"

"Not sure. Why do you ask?"

"If he was, he could have arranged for the shooter to be in place and then signaled him from his seat. Maybe he tried to negotiate with Jansen up to the last minute, but the other guy was holding all the cards. Teller goes to his seat and wrestles with the problem. He finally decides he has no choice but to take drastic action. He gives the prearranged signal to the shooter and…well, you know the rest of the story."

"A little far-fetched but possible," said Bill.

"It explains the binoculars," I added.

"It does?"

"Yup. The signal would need to be subtle, probably invisible to the naked eye from the loft."

Bill sat silent for a moment considering my theory. He slid his fedora back on his head and rubbed his eyes.

"I need to sweat Teller," he said, "or at least as much as I can without bringing the world down on me. Got anything else?"

"Take a look at a guy called Richard Purcell."

"Who's he?"

"Victor Jansen."

"What? How'd the hell did you find that out?"

"Basic shoe-leather work," I lied.

He gave me a skeptical look, started to speak, but decided against it.

"That it?" he asked.

I nodded.

"Funny thing. Teller said you had a client who was interested in this case. Are you holding anything back on me?"

"No."

The moment of truth. I reached inside my jacket for cigarettes. My Camels were soaked through. I showed them to Bill.

"Can I bum a smoke?"

He produced a pack from his coat, tapped the bottom partially ejecting one, and offered it to me. I took it. He tapped another out for himself and put it between his lips.

"Got a light? he asked.

I found my Ronson. The engraved script read Capt. Louis Rizzo, an unwelcome reminder of more honorable days. I spun the file wheel and lit the wick. My hand was quivering as I extended it towards Bill. He reached out and guided me to the target.

"When I said I needed a light, I meant my cigarette, not my nose hairs."

He knew I was lying. He was too good a cop not to. For some reason, he decided not to pursue it. We sat in silence, puffing away, lost in our private thoughts. More than once, I was tempted to come clean, but didn't.

"What's your next move?" asked Bill.

"You still want me to work this?"

"Why not? Did I miss something? You've already given me two leads I didn't have."

"Okay. You still have the photographer on ice?"

"Yup. He's all we got."

"What's his name?"

"Jake Carlson."

Can I speak to him?"

"What can you get out of him that we haven't?"

"You haven't gotten anything," I reminded him.

"Not a damn thing. Swears he's innocent, never met the victim, and never set foot in the choir loft.

"I'd like to try a different approach," I said.

"Like what?"

"I don't know. I'll just see how the conversation goes. Can you arrange it?"

"Yeah. Anything else?"

"I need to talk to the Miller family."

That was more than he could take. His face went crimson. I thought his head might explode.

"No way in hell. You stay clear of the family. They're chummy with the mayor. I don't want you speaking to any of them. You read me?"

"Loud and clear."

"All right, then. I better get home and re-introduce myself to the missus. When this mess is over, I'm gonna retire, buy myself a little place in the Ozarks, and drop off the face of the earth. Now get out of here and don't cause me any more trouble. I already have all I need."

I reached for the door handle, cracked it open, and started to leave. I turned back.

"Bill, about before…"

"Have a good night, Lou. The next round's on you. And one more thing."

"Yes?"

"Lose that damn hat."

I stepped out on to the pavement, closed the door, and watched the cruiser's red taillights as it pulled away. The rain had slowed to a drizzle. I took off the snap-brim, tossed it to the ground, and kicked it to the nearest puddle. I felt every bit the heel I was.

Chapter 15

I didn't get much sleep that night. A troubled conscience is a terrible thing to carry around sober, so I didn't try. I sat at my kitchen table with a fifth of Jack Daniels, a pack of Camels, and my one-eyed dog, Marlowe for company.

He showed up at my door a year earlier, whimpering for help, bleeding heavily from his empty right eye socket. He looked like he just lost the main event by TKO to another stray. I knew what that felt like and had to help. I poured alcohol on the wound, packed it with gauze, and bound it. He bore it all with surprising stoicism. I nursed him back to health, and he became my companion and confessor. He didn't offer much in the way of advice, but he was a good listener.

He was a brown mutt with a white blaze across his chest, and not the least bit self-conscious about his indeterminate parentage. His ears hung down across his jaws. There was a chunk missing from the left one. He's never told me how it happened, and I'm too polite to ask.

"Marlowe, you're a loyal friend. People used to be able to say that about me, and I believed it was true.

Turns out it was just another lie I've been telling myself. Bill deserves better than he's getting. He's in a bad fix. He asked for help, and I'm double-crossing him for some skirt I don't even know. It doesn't sit well with me. You understand?"

He ambled over and licked my hand. Like I said. He's a good listener.

I don't know when the booze finally dulled my conscience enough to allow me to sleep, but I woke up the next morning slumped over the table with a full ashtray and an empty bottle. Marlowe was by lying by my side. He raised his head when I stirred, his tail slowly swishing across the floor. There was no judgment in his eye. I loved that dog.

I checked my watch. It was late. Roz wasn't going to be happy. I already had to tell her I lied to Bill. I shaved and showered, fed Marlowe, and took him out for his morning relief. I buttoned up the house and headed to the office to face the music. Hopefully, it wouldn't be too loud, my head was pounding.

As I reached for the doorknob, I heard Roz's laughter coming from within. Something was tickling her fancy, which was a good thing for me. Maybe I could avoid a tirade. I turned the knob and entered. Two faces turned towards me, a scowling secretary and a tall, handsome man dressed impeccably with a smile as wide as the Mississippi and piercing gray eyes that sent the dames reeling….Picker.

"Good morning, Lou," he said, "word on the street says you're looking for me. As always, your wish is my command."

"Thanks for coming, Picker. Sorry, I'm late, hope you didn't have to wait too long."

"When you're with a beautiful woman time has no meaning."

Roz's scowl disappeared. She was glowing.

"You're not looking too well, Lou. Rough night?" he asked.

"Coffee first, questions later," I said.

"Coffee's long gone," said Roz. "You can make your own."

"I could go for another cup," said Picker.

Roz had an instant change of heart. She rose from her seat.

"I guess I could brew another pot."

The three of us filled our cups and adjourned to my office to discuss the case. Roz had already filled Picker in on the details. I gave them a report of my conversation with Bill. Roz shot me a disapproving look that promised unpleasantness later.

"What's your take on all this, Picker?" I asked.

"Classic scam gone wrong. That's the problem when you go for the big score. Too much at stake; things get ugly. In this case, we have two scams running in parallel. That means two separate marks. The first is Mercedes Miller or, more accurately, her old man..."

"...and the second is me," I said, finishing the thought for him.

"Smarter than he looks," said Picker glancing towards Roz.

"That wouldn't be too hard," she replied. "Anyway, it's not how he looks that I'm worried about; it's how he's acting."

"Can we get back to the case, please," I said.

"Well," began Picker, "the game is called a bait and cover. You've already worked out the concept. It takes a minimum of two people to pull it off, one to romance the mark, that's the bait, and another to establish a counterfeit identity, that's the cover. The cover arranges phony credentials by employing low-level hustlers to respond to phone calls at a number they provide to the mark. This Jansen guy claimed he was a financier, correct? So, the cover invents a non-existent company; let's say Continental Capital and lists the phone number on the bait's resume. Anyone doing a background check calls the number, gets a professional imposter who provides a glowing recommendation.

"For this to work, the fake references have to be in another city and the guy that answers the phone on your payroll. They need to be too distant to justify a trip to investigate. Let's say your mythical company is based in Philadelphia. The person doing the check has to ring a Philadelphia exchange, so they're half-way convinced before they even speak to anyone. The more fictitious references you can establish, the stronger the con. It's more expensive but worth the price if the prize is big enough. The goal is to limit the background check to phone inquiries. Most calls are delegated to an assistant or secretary. The primary doesn't get involved unless there is a suspicion of fraud."

"You'd have to know a lot of hustlers in a lot of towns," I said.

"Not a problem for career cons. They've probably worked this game in cities all over the country. They would make it a point to establish professional contacts in all of them.

"The next step, as you have already suggested, is the shakedown. Your initial assumption that the threat of family humiliation gives the bait all the leverage he needs is one possibility. A second, sometimes more effective, form of leverage comes from the threat of going through with the marriage. A simple ultimatum...pay me now or pay me for the rest of your life. Most marks will fold their hand and be done with it, but every now-and-then, one will resist. In that case, there's only one solution."

"A lump of lead," I said.

"Or an unfortunate accident," added Roz.

"Or a pair of concrete wing-tips and a stroll in the river," said Picker with a smile. "That's why the bait waits until the last minute for the shakedown. It doesn't give the mark sufficient time to plan any foul play."

"Did anything in the police file catch your attention?" I asked.

"There are some oddities, but there always are. All the evidence seems to fit the scenario."

"What is my client after."

"Beats me, but I guarantee you it has nothing to do with revenge."

"If you think she's the cover, then there would be no need for another partner," said Roz.

"Beauty and brains. You've got a gem here, Lou."

She blushed redder than a stoplight. If Picker didn't pull back the throttle, she was going to blow a gasket. He changed the subject.

"Did you see something in the police photos we didn't?" he said.

"Yes, Let's have another look at those loft photos," I replied.

Roz fished them out and laid them in front of us.

"Anything jump out at either of you?" I asked?

"The binoculars," said Roz.

"Yes, that's an oddity, but one we can account for. Don't look at the individual objects. Step back and take in the whole scene. There's got to be something we're missing."

Picker shook his head.

"Darned if I see anything."

"Me neither," said Roz.

"I don't either, but I've got a gut feeling the answer is right before our eyes. Well, we can't sit around and speculate. We need to get a plan of action."

"What do you want us to do next, Lou?" asked Picker.

"I'd like you to turn over a few stones and see what your associates know about the Purcells. Somebody in your circles may have run across them."

"I can do that, but you know Purcell probably isn't their real name."

"I don't expect it is."

"Are you suggesting your client might be lying?" asked Roz.

That road led nowhere, so I changed direction.

"I'm going to interview the alleged shooter after lunch, but I'd like to get a crack at the Millers."

"You can't do that!" interjected Roz. "You're going to get Bill fired. He ruled out any contact with them."

"That he did, but he didn't say anything about you. Want to give it a shot?"

Her concern for Bill vanished as quickly as a pork chop in a wolves' den. This is what she'd been waiting for since she threw in with me.

"You bet, boss! How do I go about it?"

"I bet Picker can dream up something if you ask him nicely."

"I've got a few ideas already," he said. "Let's put our heads together, beautiful, and see what we can come up with."

Roz was in favor of that

Chapter 16

It was a short ride to the precinct where the alleged shooter was in the slammer. The desk sergeant surveyed me dispassionately. He saw worse every day. I gave him my name and told him I was there to see Lt. Newton. He shrugged, picked up his phone, and rang Bill's office.

"There's a derelict here to see you. Says his name is Rizzo."

Bill appeared in short order. He assessed my sleep-deprived, hungover, countenance.

"Jeez, Rizzo. You get the number of the truck that hit you?"

"Funny. Can one of you fine public servants spare some aspirin for a taxpayer?"

Bill turned to the sergeant. "Wilson, you got anything behind the desk?"

The uniform reached under the counter and produced a bottle of pills. I took it, shook out a few, and swallowed them dry.

Bill motioned me to follow, then led me down a hall and past the holding cells. He went to a door at the end of the hallway and down a flight of stairs. At the bottom was a solitary cell behind a solid door with a small, barred opening. Sitting on a cot and staring at the ceiling was a rangy fellow with a blonde crewcut. He wore denim shirt and trousers that were too big for him. He needed a shave and a good night's sleep. He glanced at me through the opening in the door with no apparent interest.

"You got a visitor, Jake," said Newton.

He looked at me again.

"Don't know him," he muttered. "He another cop?"

"Nope."

"A new mouthpiece? Gotta be an improvement over the one I got."

"No. He's a private dick who's working for a client that has an interest in the case. You willing to talk to him? I'll go upstairs; there will be no cops around. What have you got to lose? We've got an eyewitness that puts you at the crime scene. Thing's ain't looking too good for you right now. Maybe this guy can help."

"You got a smoke?" he asked me.

I nodded.

"What the hell, let him in."

When we were alone, I tapped out a butt and offered it to him.

"What's your story?" he asked as he fished it from the pack.

I tapped one out for myself and lit us both. I planned to gain his confidence, hoping he might see me as an ally and drop his guard. We sat in silence for a few moments puffing away.

"My name is Lou Rizzo. I've got a client who thinks the cops have this whole thing wrong. I agree. It's all a little too neat for my liking. The question is how'd the real bad guys settle on you as the patsy?"

"I've been sitting here for days trying to figure that out. Maybe I'm just unlucky."

"You wouldn't be the first guy in the wrong place at the wrong time."

"If you're trying to make me feel better, it ain't working," he said allowing himself a half-smile. That was a good sign.

"I suppose not."

He eyed me, seeming to notice my patch for the first time.

"What happened to you?"

"Couple of rounds through the cockpit of my B-25."

"Tough break."

"Maybe I'm unlucky too."

"I got one in the leg," he said patting his right thigh, "never been one hundred percent since. Seen a lot of good men splattered all over France, so I can't really complain."

"Where'd it happen?"

"Bastogne, December '44, 101st Airborne, 506th Regiment."

"Bloody."

"Cold as hell too."

"Straight-leg infantry?"

"Medic, at least at the start. By the end, I had run out of drugs and bandages, so I took off my medic's armband and grabbed a rifle."

"Where you from, Jake?"

"I was from Iowa before the war. The family had a farm; always thought I'd be a farmer too. Gave it a good try when I got back, but I was a different guy. I'd seen too much. Did you think you'd be a private eye?"

"Nope, had other plans but they didn't pan out."

"Always liked cameras," he continued. "Thought I might give the news business a try. Couldn't catch on with the *Des Moines Register* but managed to make a few bucks as an independent. I thought the grass might be greener here, a bigger town with more papers, so I packed up and moved."

"How long you been a stringer?"

"Off and on about a year, but as I said, I'm new in town. Been here a couple of weeks. Haven't sold a damn thing. Thought a couple of good society wedding shots might jump-start my career. Doesn't seem to be working out too well."

"Know anybody else working the wedding?"

"A few familiar faces but no names. It's a competitive game."

"Cops say no one can place you at the time of the shooting."

"We're pretty good at blending into the background."

"Guess so," I said. "Want another smoke."

"Don't mind if I do."

We each took a few drags on our new smokes, then I pressed on.

"You know the Millers?"

"Nope."

"Did anyone approach you to plug the groom."

"Nope."

"I don't imagine you'd tell me if anyone did."

"I said I was shot in the leg, not the head."

"The important thing is that my client thinks you're being framed. I'll keep digging and see if we can spring you. If you think of anything I can use, tell Newton you want to speak to Rizzo. I've got to say you don't seem too nervous for a guy looking at the death penalty."

"They got nothing on me except the word of some old broad loopy on ether. I was a medic, remember? Assisted in some surgeries. I know how that stuff works."

"A word of advice, brother. I don't think I'd mention that again," I said.

That brought an abrupt end to the conversation. Jake puffed in silence, no doubt cursing himself for letting his guard down. We finished our cigarettes about the time Newton returned.

"You ladies finish your tea?" he asked.

"Got all I need," I said.

As we left, Jake offered a mock salute. "Thanks for the smokes," he said.

I tossed him the rest of the pack. Bill and I didn't speak until we reached the top of the stairs. We made our way to his office, a sparsely appointed, windowless room about the size of a broom closet. He settled into a chair behind a metal table that served as his desk. A telephone, notepad, and coffee cup provided the ambiance. He motioned me to a metal chair opposite him.

"Coffee?" he asked.

"No thanks."

"Well, what do you think of our suspect."

"No alibi, but the perfect backstory."

"Tell me something I don't know."

"Did you tell him there were no prints at the scene?"

"No. Why?"

"He says he's not worried because you have nothing on him. How would he know there were no prints unless he's the one who wiped them?"

"He'd know if he wasn't there," said Bill.

"That's one explanation. Tell me this, did you check his military record?"

"Yeah, the guy was a medic. Took one in the leg somewhere in Europe. That's why he limps. Surprising, since the Geneva Convention makes firing at a medic a war crime."

"Wouldn't be the first time the convention was ignored."

"No, I guess not."

"It also prevents them from carrying a weapon," I said. "but I never saw a medic without a pistol."

"What does that have to do with the case?"

"We need to establish if our pal Jake had the chops to take the shot from the loft."

"Not with a pistol, nobody does."

"Everybody trains with a rifle at infantry school. See if you can give those pencil jockeys at the Pentagon a swift kick in the brass and get his records. We need to know if he qualified as a marksman. If he did, you've got two legs of the triple crown...means, and opportunity. You'd still need a motive, but you might be able to use the new info to sweat him."

"Might work. I'll get on it. Anything else?"

"He told me a fish story about running out of medical supplies, stripping off his armband and grabbing a rifle. Never heard of a guy doing that."

"Which proves what?"

"He likes to shoot things."

Chapter 17

The next day, Picker and Roz were back in the office. I could tell she was pleased with herself and eager to make her report. We drank coffee, smoked cigarettes, and compared notes. I went first, and they listened with interest.

Next came Picker who reported that, after a few dead ends, he was able to unearth an interesting nugget. An out-of-town associate was familiar with a husband and wife bunco team with the same M.O.

"Did you say wife?" asked Roz.

"Yup, a redhead," he added, "a looker."

"My, my," she clucked shooting me her you're-an-idiot glance.

"Anything else?" I asked.

"He went by the name of Charles Morgan. The wife was Donna. They fleeced the family of a socialite in Dallas out of twenty grand. Looks like they upped the ante with the Millers. Got greedy and paid the price."

"That's interesting," I said, "but doesn't tell us anything helpful."

"Patience, my friend. I've got a little more legwork to do."

"What have you been up to?" I asked Roz.

"I have an appointment tomorrow with Mercedes Miller. Her father and brother will be there also"

"How'd you manage that?" I asked in amazement.

"It was Picker's plan. It seems that before his death, Victor Jansen took out a one hundred-thousand-dollar life insurance policy naming Mrs. Mercedes Jansen as beneficiary. The policy was in effect at the time of his death, but there is no Mrs. Jansen, so some details have to be cleared up before the policy can be paid. As a representative of the insurance company, I will be meeting with the Millers at their residence at 10 AM tomorrow to validate the beneficiary's claim on the payout."

"Good work," I said.

"Don't thank me. Thank Picker. The question is: what am I looking for?"

"You're looking for a chink in the armor."

"Like what?"

"Did the old man suspect he was being conned? If so, when did he get wise? How about Junior? Was he worried about being ousted at Miller's Lumber? I can't tell you exactly how to proceed. That will depend on how each reacts. You're on a fishing expedition. Throw some chum in the water and see what slithers up from deep."

"Got it, Chief."

"Don't forget the grieving fiancée," added Picker. If they get a whiff of betrayal, women can be very dangerous. Of course, they're all dangerous to begin with," he said eyeing Roz.

"Why don't you come with me?" she asked Picker. "I could use the help."

"I don't make house calls; at least not when the occupants are present. The fewer people that can identify me, the better. I have business outside this case."

"Look," I said, "why don't you two work out a more detailed plan of attack for the Millers. See if Picker can polish up your act. I'm going to have a chat with Reverend Fletcher at Riverfront Christian."

"You figure he knows something?" asked Picker.

"If you were a killer-for-hire, instead of a petty thief you wouldn't have to ask that question," I said.

"I'm substantial by nature, petty by choice," he said feigning insult.

"A professional shooter," I continued, "wouldn't just show up and pull the trigger. He'd case the place first, looking for the best place to take the shot and plan an escape route. Maybe the Reverend or his staff saw a suspicious stranger wandering around."

"Worth a shot," observed Picker.

I grabbed my coat and hat and was headed for the door when a thought came to me.

"Roz, is the autopsy report in that stack of paperwork that Newton gave us?"

"No, but it's been less than a week. Besides, the cause of death is hardly in doubt."

Chapter 18

The ornate wooden doors of Riverfront Christian were unlocked and swung open silently at my urging. It was an impressive columned structure with marble floors leading to a slightly elevated altar flanked by a hand-carved pulpit. A set of stairs off the entrance led to the loft.

I made my way up the stairs to the landing where the cops found the rifle, paused a moment to look around, but there was nothing to see. I climbed the last bit to the loft and surveyed the scene. All the evidence had long since been removed. I peered over the loft rail. It was the perfect perch for a sniper. I paced back and forth trying to re-create what had happened that fateful day. I went through several scenarios, but none fit the circumstances better than Mrs. Clayborn's account.

I moved down the stairs and walked to the altar, my footsteps echoing through the vacant hall. I reached the altar and located the approximate spot where Jansen had fallen. The marble flooring had been scrubbed clean leaving no trace of the violence that had taken place. I was about to call out in the hope of getting someone's attention when I heard loud voices coming from a room on the left side of the church abeam the altar.

The voices, one male and one female, were angry. I hadn't noticed them until now, so the conversation must have just recently heated up. The door opened and a middle-aged woman scurried out, closing the door behind her. She made brief eye contact with me, then lowered her eyes and walked to the far end of the church where she opened another door, letting in the sunlight. She stepped through and was gone.

The argument continued. I walked toward the voices. As I got closer to the room, I saw a placard labeled *Riverfront Christian Church, Reverend Chester A. Fletcher, Pastor.* I leaned in towards the door to make out what was being said at the very moment the door swung open smacking me in the kisser. Another middle-aged woman burst out. She wore a flowered print dress, white hat, and gloves and carried a white purse. She looked vaguely familiar. She gave me a cursory glance then stormed off without so much as an apology.

A man with a shock of silver hair and wearing a clerical collar followed her out. He was visibly upset and called after her.

"Abigail, wait. Please, we can work this out."

It fell on deaf ears. When he turned to go back to his office, he finally noticed me. At first, he appeared disoriented but quickly regained his footing.

"How may I help you, my son?"

"I'm not exactly sure," I replied. "Are you Reverend Fletcher?"

"Yes, I am. And you would be?"

"Lou Rizzo, I'm a private investigator working for a client with an interest in the Jansen murder."

That visibly upset him, but he recovered his pastoral demeanor.

"Terrible thing, but I've already told the police everything I know…several times."

"If you could just spare me a few minutes, it would mean a great deal."

"I'm sorry, but I have nothing to add. You need to talk to the police."

"That woman who just left seemed familiar. Where do I know her from?"

"You're not a member of the congregation, are you?"

"No. Why?"

"If you were, you'd know she's our organist and choir director, Abigail Clayborn."

"The one that got drugged the day of the murder. I remember reading about that in the paper. Kinda struck me as odd."

"Odd? How so?"

"Big deal wedding like that, but no choir."

"Nothing odd about it. The bride elected to go with a soloist, but she took ill at the last moment, and we had to do without?"

"Before the wedding, did you notice any strangers hanging around here?"

"This is a house of God; all are welcome."

"Did you see any unauthorized people in the loft?"

"No."

"It's none of my business, but what was Mrs. Clayborn so angry about?"

"You're right. It's church business and none of yours. Now, if you'll excuse me. I have work to do. Feel free to stay and worship as you choose. I assume you can find your way out. Have a good day and may God bless you, my son."

There wasn't anything else I could do. I made my way out into the street. The sun had disappeared behind a gray blanket of water-laden clouds. Rain was imminent. My stomach growled, reminding me I hadn't eaten all day. I remembered passing a diner about two blocks away and headed for it. I sat down at the counter and ordered a burger and a coffee. I was about half-way through my meal when a short, muscular guy with slicked-back hair and a cauliflower ear took the seat next to me. Since I was the only other customer in the joint, that seemed a little unusual.

He sat down and opened the conversation.

"Lou Rizzo, isn't it?"

I'd never laid an eye on the guy before. He had the hard, smug look of hired muscle.

"Maybe I am and maybe I'm not. What's it to you?"

"Nothing much. I got a message for you."

"There's a post office down the street. Why don't you drop me a line?"

I went back to my sandwich. He grabbed me by the shoulder and spun me towards him. His suit jacket opened as he reached out, revealing a shoulder holster and a piece.

"No reason to be rude," he said.

He grabbed the heavy glass sugar dispenser and twirled it in his hand.

"They say you can catch more flies with sugar than vinegar."

"So, what's the message?"

"Thought you'd never ask," he said reaching in the side pocket of his jacket.

He retrieved a small piece of paper folded neatly in half and slid it across the counter. As I reached for it, he slammed the dispenser down across my knuckles. The pain came hot and fast, accompanied by a show of stars in front of my face. I pulled the injured hand to my chest. He grabbed me by the lapels, lifted me up, and drew me towards him.

"Here's the message. Stay away from the Jansen case."

He flung me back in my seat.

"Enjoy the rest of your meal."

To the counterman, who had recognized trouble. and given us a wide berth, he said. "I think the one-eyed-jack could use some ice."

Chapter 19

The counterman did his best to nurse my hand. He put some ice in a towel, placed my hand inside it, and used my tie to secure it in place. It hurt like the devil. I thanked and paid him, then retraced my steps to where I had parked the Merc. It was raining again, adding to my misery. My left hand was throbbing. I was able to control the steering wheel with a combination of my forearm and knee allowing me to shift normally with my right.

I drove to the city hospital where they x-rayed me and pronounced I had three broken bones. They put me in a cast and gave me some painkillers.

"What happened to you?" the doctor asked.

"Slammed it in a car door," I replied.

He gave me a skeptical look.

"I get a lot of cases like that."

I managed to get home where Marlowe was waiting patiently for my return. I let him out to perform his ablutions and headed for the kitchen cabinet where I kept a couple of bottles of whiskey. There would be one less come morning. I put some food and fresh water in Marlowe's bowl and whistled him in. That was the last I remember.

I was dreaming of a romantic interlude with Lana Turner where she was smothering me with kisses. Turns out it was only Marlowe coaxing me awake to tend to his needs. The pounding in my head was a pleasant distraction from the pain in my hand. I stumbled to the kitchen, found the jar of painkillers, and downed twice the recommended dosage. Going to the office was out of the question, so I headed back to bed and was soon out cold.

I don't know how long I was in my drug and alcohol-induced coma, but when I woke up, I wasn't alone. I heard sounds coming from the kitchen. I reached in my nightstand and pulled out my little Smith and Wesson pistol. With an unsteady hand, I aimed it at the bedroom door intent on shooting whoever came through. When I heard footsteps approaching, I drew the hammer back. The bad news was the barrel was wobbling; the good news was I was seeing double, which increased the probability of hitting something. When a man came through the threshold, I squeezed the trigger. The hammer fell, but nothing happened. I squeezed again with the same results.

"You might need these," said a familiar voice.

The double images started to merge, revealing Picker's smiling face. His right hand was extended, palm upward, revealing six, .22 caliber slugs.

"A drunk and his ammo are soon parted," he said.

My hand was throbbing in rhythm to the beating of my heart. The tips of my fingers that were visible under the cast were a combination of green and purple. The hand was badly swollen; it felt like the cast was about two sizes too small.

"Pills," was all I could muster.

Picker had the coffee going in the pot and steak and eggs frying in the pan. I sat at the kitchen table praying the pills would take effect. Picker poured me a cup of coffee, ordered me to drink it, and went back to the stove.

"What are you doing here?" I asked.

"Looking for you. No one's heard from you all day. You didn't come to the office, didn't answer the phone, and then I got word on the street that some guy with a patch had trouble at a local diner. I figured you might need some help. A wounded animal always returns to its lair, so I started here. Sure enough, your car was parked out front. I knocked; no one answered. I let myself in."

"I'm pretty sure I turned the deadbolt before I crashed."

"You did."

"How long did it take?"

"Twenty seconds. I'm slowing down in my old age."

"What about the dog? I didn't hear him bark," I said giving Marlowe a stern look. He whimpered and put his head between his paws.

"You didn't hear the phone ring either?"

"Maybe I heard it. Can't say. Don't care."

He plated the steak and eggs and slid it in front of me. He took a second plate for himself. We ate in silence playing a game of verbal chicken. I blinked first.

"Aren't you going to ask me?"

"Okay. I'll ask. How do you like my cooking?"

"Damn it, Picker. You know what I mean."

"There's nothing to ask. Your investigation touched a raw nerve. You were warned off. Had to be Teller or someone he works for. Couldn't be the Reverend; he wouldn't have had enough time to set it up. How bad is the hand?"

"Three broken bones. Forget about that; I need to get to the office and see what Roz turned up with the Millers."

"You're not going to find out today. It's 5 PM."

"I've been out all day?"

I shook my head. That was a mistake. The cannons in my head started going off.

"Finish your dinner, grab a shower, and get a goodnight's sleep. We'll see what Roz turned up tomorrow. I'll spend the night on your sofa. Marlowe and I will stand watch in case your pal from the diner decides you need an encore performance."

Chapter 20

"What happened to your hand?" asked Roz.

"Had an altercation with a sugar dispenser."

"I take it you lost."

"Never mind that. How'd it go with the Millers?"

"Well, in my opinion..."

"Save the opinion for later," I interrupted. "For now, let's go with the facts starting at the beginning."

"Have it your way," she sniffed. "I arrived at The Arbor, that's the Miller manse just west of town, at 10 AM. A butler answered the door. I introduced myself as Patricia Bolton from Wellington Life Insurance Company and that I had an appointment. He said Mr. Miller was expecting me, motioned to follow, and ushered me into an opulent office off the dining room. The old man was seated at a polished mahogany desk. His daughter was seated in a wing chair to his right. She was wearing a ruby dress, matching heels, and lipstick, not your traditional widow's weeds. I gave her a pass because, technically, she wasn't a widow. Junior was standing behind her. Their attorney was also present, a bookish man with spectacles who eyed me with suspicion. His name was Robertson."

"I offered my credentials, counterfeit documents Picker secured for me. When everyone was satisfied with my credentials, I launched into my story. The attorney asked if my company ever had a similar case. I answered we had, but this case had a twist; the policyholder didn't just die, he was murdered. Until a final police report was issued vindicating the beneficiary and her family, the company would be withholding payment. That didn't sit too well with Senior and Junior or their lawyer who loudly proclaimed their outrage. Mercedes seemed disinterested."

"I said surely they could understand why my company found the circumstances peculiar. The Miller's obviously were a family of means. Why would Mr. Jansen feel the need to ensure his own life and name his wife...excuse me, Miss Miller as the beneficiary? The lawyer jumped all over that, saying the fact that they didn't need the money set the family above suspicion."

"I inquired if an autopsy had been performed. Senior got belligerent and asked if suffered a head injury recently and pointed out the obvious cause of death. I assured him it was simply another document which needed to be added to the file. I asked when the funeral was planned. They exchanged furtive glances. I thought that odd. No one said anything until the attorney admitted that the body had not been claimed."

"I asked if they did their due diligence before the wedding. The lawyer said they had. Mercedes's demeanor switched from disinterest to aggravation. She said love was all the due diligence she needed. Senior shook his head in disgust. He said he hired a detective firm which gave Jansen a clean bill of health."

"Next, I asked if there was some sort of prenuptial agreement. The lawyer objected on the basis of confidentiality. Mercedes said she didn't need or want one. I loaded up and threw my haymaker. Did any of them have reason to want Jansen dead? That brought Senior to his feet. He pounded his fist on the desk and bellowed obscenities at me. Junior restrained him while eyeing me with murderous intent. Mercedes blurted *they both did* and fled the room."

"The attorney jumped in explaining that Miss Miller was under a terrible strain, was being sedated, and that nothing she said could be taken seriously. He added that the Millers had given their statements to the police, and they were done discussing the case.

Senior was still agitated and ordered me out of the house. It seemed like a good idea, so I complied. As I made my way out, he yelled to me that he would be making a formal complaint to my boss."

"He's in for a shock," said Picker. "That number we gave him on your bogus business card connects to my barber."

"That's all very interesting," I said, "but what do we know now that we didn't know before?" I asked.

"I think Senior's involved," said Roz. "The insurance story put him off his game. He was rattled by the thought that another investigation might be launched."

"What do you make of Mercedes's statement that both her father and brother wanted Jansen dead?" I said.

"We already knew there might be some animus from Junior based on his fear of being displaced. Senior, on the other hand, had only one possible reason; Jansen had already made his play," said Picker.

"What about Mercedes? Why no mourning clothes?" I asked. "*The Lady in Red* routine doesn't fit."

"She's probably in shock," said Roz. "I guess her father told her about the shakedown, but she didn't believe it and insisted on going through with the wedding. So, Senior decided to make the problem go away. Mercedes couldn't handle it. Maybe, part of her thinks he isn't dead."

"Would Senior have had enough time to set the whole thing up?" I asked.

"*Res ipsa loquitir*," she said.

"Huh?"

"It's Latin: *The thing speaks for itself.* Jansen's in the morgue," she explained.

I turned to Picker. "What about you? Got any thoughts?"

"What made you add that bit about the autopsy?" asked Picker. "That wasn't something we discussed."

"I don't know," said Roz. "Seemed like a good idea at the time."

"The old man didn't like the question, did he?" asked Picker.

"Is it significant?" she asked.

"It is," he replied, "if they claim the body tomorrow."

Chapter 21

I congratulated Roz on a job well done. She had stirred the pot. For now, there was nothing more to do until the ingredients settled. No new suspect had emerged, but none had been eliminated either. Was their behavior all that suspicious? Experience told me the elite class was populated by more oddballs than skid row. The difference between eccentric and crazy is a bank account.

In the meantime, I had a lead I wanted to follow-up on.

"Roz, does the police report have the organist's address?"

"Yes, I'm pretty sure I saw it somewhere." She went over to her desk and rifled through the papers. After a minute,
she announced she found it. She scribbled it down on a piece of paper and handed it to me.

"Thanks. I think I'll pay the lady a visit. Maybe I can jog her memory."

Abigail Clayborn lived in a modest craftsman style home in Richmond Heights. I arrived just before lunch and went up the white wooden stairs to the front porch where two wicker rocking chairs sat idly on either side of a wooden table. The early fall foliage was beginning to work its magic on the maples and poplars that filled the yard. I called ahead to make sure she was home, hanging up when she answered. I didn't want her expecting me. People are easier to work when they're caught off-guard. I rang the bell.

The woman who I saw leaving Reverend Fletcher's office in a huff answered the door. As she had yesterday, she wore a floral print dress. Her dark hair was sprinkled with gray. She checked me over and I saw a glimmer of recognition in her brown eyes.

"You're the gentleman who was in the church yesterday when Reverend Fletcher and I were finishing up our conversation."

"That was me. You seemed upset."

"Did I? Well, I'm passionate about what I do. What can I do for you, Mister...uh, what did you say your name was?"

"Rizzo...Lou Rizzo. I'm a private investigator. My client has an interest in the Jansen murder, so I was hoping to ask you a couple of questions. Can you spare me a few minutes?"

She thought about that for a moment, hesitated, then motioned to one of the wicker rockers.

"I was just making some tea; would you like a cup?"

I would have preferred a bourbon, but that's not the afternoon beverage of choice for suburban ladies. At least not in public.

"That would be very nice."
She disappeared into the house and returned with tea service and cookies. She had donned a sweater against the slight chill.

"Mr. Rizzo, I wish I could help you, but I told the police everything I know."

"I'm sure you did, but I was hoping a question or two might jog your memory."

"I suppose it can't hurt, if you think it will help."

"Thank you. How long have you worked at Riverfront?"

"About three years. I started when my husband died. A wonderful man. I needed the money to keep up with expenses. Reverend Fletcher hired me as the musical director. I work with the choir and play the organ. Or rather I did. He dismissed me yesterday. That's what the argument you witnessed was about."

"What happened?"

"It's personal."

"Sorry, I didn't mean to intrude."

"It's not your concern, young man."

"No, it's not. Had you ever seen the shooter before the incident?"

"No, of course not, and I barely saw him then. I was too busy to take much notice."

"But you did notice the limp."

"Yes, it was just one of those little details that stuck in my mind."

"I'm told the soloist called in sick at the eleventh hour."

"Yes, it left us in an awkward situation."

"Is she any good?"

"I've worked with better, but she's adequate and normally reliable."

"Do you have her address or phone number handy?"

"I don't feel comfortable divulging that."

"No matter. That's enough business. What did your husband do?"

"He managed a grocery store, but his sideline was his passion. He was a backwoods Ozark guide."

"I'm glad he got the opportunity."

"I'm thankful every day," she said wistfully. "Some of my fondest memories are hiking and hunting in the woods together."

I grabbed my fedora and stood up.

"Thank you for your time, Mrs. Clayborn. I hope you land on your feet."

"That's very kind of you, Mr. Rizzo. I hope I was of some help. As I said, I gave a thorough statement to the police. Losing my job is a terrible blow. I was barely scraping by before I was let go. I'm already behind in my house payments."

Chapter 22

I wanted to talk to the soloist, but I also needed to head to the Mayfair and have a chat with my client. I stopped at a gas station and used the payphone to ring Anne's room. I told her I'd be there in an hour. We arranged to meet in the dining room for an early dinner.

I hung up, checked the directory for Riverfront Christian, and placed a second call. I got the parish secretary. I told her I was planning a wedding and looking for a good soloist. Word was the woman they used was the best. I asked for her name and phone number and wrote down the information on the back of my business card. Her name was Sophie Fromm, and she lived in Clayton, just west of the city.

I dialed her number, and she answered on the third ring.

"Fromm residence."

"Yes ma'am, my name is Lou Rizzo, and I'm investigating the Jansen murder. You may have read about it."

"Of course, I have. I was wondering when the police would get around to me."

If she thought I was a cop, I saw no reason to correct her.

"Better late than never. Do you remember approximately what time you called in sick that day?"

"I'm afraid I don't know what you're talking about. I wasn't sick. Abigail Clayborn called and told me to stay home. She said a Miller family friend had flown in from New York as a surprise. She was a childhood friend of the bride and wanted the honor of performing at the wedding. Abigail told me she was a musical theater student and was quite good. Not as good as me but there was nothing she could do about it."

"That's show business," I said. "Thank you for your help. You'll be hearing from us again."

"Before you go, may I ask you a question."

"Fire away."

"Have you seen Chet since the shooting? I can't seem to reach him."

"Chet?"

"I'm sorry, Reverend Fletcher."

"I've seen him once. Why do you ask?"

"This whole mess must be quite a shock for him," she replied.

"I'm sure it is."

I got back in the Merc and headed to the office. I was a few minutes out when an unmarked cruiser pulled up alongside me. Two plainclothesmen were inside. The driver flashed his badge and motioned me to pull over. The cop in the passenger seat got out and came over to my window. I'd seen him before but couldn't recall his name.

"Hey, Rizzo. How's it going?"

"Fine, but I'm in kind of a rush. Got plans."

"Plans change. Newton wants to see you."

"Now?"

"Ten minutes ago. Follow us."

The boys turned on the siren, and we sped through the city. We were headed in the direction of Sportsman Park which meant our destination was the Warning Track. I wondered what could be so urgent that Bill would track me down in the middle of the day. I wondered if Roz's visit to the Millers had already brought the house down on him. I also wondered what I would tell Anne. She didn't strike me as the type of woman who was accustomed to being stood-up, but there wasn't much I could do about it.

The place was a lot quieter at lunch than dinner and much better lit. Bill was sitting in his favorite spot. He motioned me over, and I slid into the booth.

He was drinking coffee and eating a ham sandwich; he had a splotch of mustard on the corner of his mouth. I touched a pinkie to my lips in the universal gesture. He grunted, grabbed the faded napkin off his lap, and wiped it away.

"Better?" he asked.

"Much, now you can go to the prom."

"Want something to eat?" he asked.

"I'm here. Might as well."

Bill held up the remains of his sandwich and hailed the bartender.

"Hey Smokey, bring my friend one of these and a cup of coffee."

He noticed the cast on my hand.

"What happened to you?"

"Some punk smashed it with a sugar dispenser at a diner. He said it was a message from his boss to stay away from the Jansen case. He didn't mention who his boss was. As far as messages go, I thought it was overkill. A phone call would have done it."

"Sounds like you struck a nerve somewhere."

"I guess that's why you're considered the pride of the force."

Bill shrugged that off and got down to business.

"You making any progress on your end?" he asked.

"I don't know if you can call it progress, but I do have some new dope for you."

"Let's hear it."

"Did you know there was supposed to be a soloist at the wedding that day?"

"Yeah. She called in sick at the last minute. Got anything I don't already know?"

"The soloist wasn't sick."

"And you know that because?"

"She told me. You'd be surprised what you can find out by just asking."

"Then, why didn't she show?"

"Clayborn called her and said she wouldn't be needed."

"Why would she do that?"

"I don't know, but I'll tell you something else. Clayborn is broke which means she could have been bought-off to turn a blind eye and allow herself to be drugged. That wouldn't have been feasible with another person in the loft."

"Oh, one other thing. Clayborn said Fletcher fired her yesterday, a fact he failed to mention when I spoke to him. The two of them were in a heated argument when I visited the church yesterday afternoon."

"Did either say what it was about?"

"Both said it was personal. She's a widow. What's Fletcher's situation?"

"Widower," said Bill, "been one for a few years. I'm not sure if the firing means anything at all, but I'll give you this, the timing is curious."

"Fromm, the soloist referred to Fletcher as *Chet*. I thought that was a little chummy."

Bill raised an eyebrow. "Anything else?"

I started to tell him about Roz's visit with the Millers, but before I got the first sentence out, he flew into a rage. Bits of sandwich and spittle flew from his mouth as he bellowed every obscenity known to man and some new ones I think he made up on the spot. The two plainclothesmen who had brought me in were seated at the far end of the bar. They got up and approached us.

"Everything okay here, boss," asked the guy who had been driving.

"Just peachy," he said waving them back to the bar.

He turned back to me.

"I told you to stay clear of the Millers. The brass is going to pull down my drawers and hang me from the flagpole."

"I didn't get within ten city blocks of them," I offered in protest. "You didn't say anything about my associates. Sorry, if I misunderstood you. You want to hear the story or not?"

"Damage is done, might as well."

I gave him the whole duffle bag-full and waited while he chewed it over.

"Funny that the autopsy came up," he finally said.

"Why?"

"That's why I had my guys pick you up. The coroner's report came in. The cause of death was obvious, but here's the interesting part; he was already a dead man walking. His body contained lethal levels of arsenic. I guess somebody wanted to make damn sure he was dead."

"Or two people wanted him out of the way," I added.

"Yeah, thought of that. Here's another interesting item; Mercedes Miller claimed the body as soon as the coroner released it." He looked at his watch. "It was cremated an hour ago."

"That puts the focus squarely on the Millers," I said, "but which one?"

"That's the jackpot question, isn't it? You been looking under any other rocks?"

"My source, who is wise to the criminal element, says a pair of scammers have been working the wealthy heiress market in major cities."

"Now, that's a real nugget. How reliable is your source?"

"Gold plated. He says they went by the names of Charles and Donna Morgan when they were working a mark in Dallas. You might want to check with the Dallas cops; see what they've got."

"Gee, Sherlock, I never would have thought of that. So, the silent partner's a dame. You know anything about her?"

It was the perfect opportunity to come clean about my client, clear my conscience, and get out of the hole I was digging for myself. Instead, I reached for the shovel.

"Nothing."

"You're dealing me off the bottom of the deck. I've tolerated it so far, but my patience is wearing thin."

I checked my watch. I could still make my dinner date if I hurried.

"Bill, I've got somewhere I need to be. I'll catch up with you if anything else turns up. I slid out of the booth. Bill held up a finger indicating for me to hold on a second."

"Three things, Sherlock. Number one, I know you're holding out on me. Number two, The Army confirmed Carlson qualified as a marksman."

"And Number three?"

"Next time, it's your turn to buy."

Chapter 23

I was fifteen minutes late arriving at the Mayfair. I headed straight for the bar. Anne was the only customer there. She was wearing a beige suit and brown, saddle shoe pumps. She was working on a martini, a cigarette, and acting enthralled by my bartender buddy.

"Sorry I'm late," I said. "I got pulled over by the cops."

"What for?" she asked.

"Brake light out. Anyway, I'm sorry I kept you waiting."

"I didn't even notice. I was enjoying my conversation with Tommy. Did you know he was a war hero? The Jerrys tried to blow him up with a cannon. Can you believe it?"

Tommy was sporting a grin that made the Cheshire Cat seem like he was suffering from depression.

"Amazing," I said, "did he offer to show you his scar?"

"Don't be vulgar, Louis," she reprimanded me. "Shall we go to the dining room. They're holding a table for us."

We were seated, handed menus, and placed our drink orders. Roz couldn't object. It was after business hours.

"What happened to your hand?"

"Broke a nail thumbing through files, occupational hazard."

She gave me a go-to-hell look.

"You arranged this meeting," she said. "I assume I am finally going to get some information for my investment."

"Well, Anne, or is it Donna?"

She shrugged non-committedly, betraying nothing. You wouldn't want to get in a poker game with this dame. "Whatever you like. I'm impressed. Where did you dig that up?"

"Doll, you hired the best dick in the city. Here's some more whipped cream for your sundae. Your brother or husband or whoever the hell he was, died from a gunshot wound, but he would have been dead in a matter of hours anyway. Someone served him an arsenic cocktail."

She remained impassive. She reached for her purse, pulled out a silver cigarette case and a mother-of-pearl holder. She looked to me for a light, and I obliged. She inhaled the first puff and exhaled a nicely formed ring through pursed lips. The waiter took our order, a Cobb salad for her, and another whiskey for me.

"We know," she began, "how he died or how he was going to die, but we still don't know who the murderer or murderers were. All you've done is double my problem. Now there are two people I have to kill."

"At the rate we're going, you'll need a hunting license," I quipped.

"Who are your main suspects?" she asked.

"I'm focusing on the Millers, Senior and Junior, but I haven't ruled out Mercedes. Then, of course, there is you."

She didn't react. I was like a boxer who just threw his best haymaker but missed. When the waiter arrived with her salad, she pushed it aside, leaned forward with her elbows on the table, and gestured at me with her cigarette. Her voice was firm, but the volume was measured.

"What would be my motive for killing my partner?"

"Revenge for double-crossing you and marrying the mark. Or suppose he wasn't your brother, but a lover. The green-eyed monster is a nasty beast. Take yours, for example, they're beautiful but cold as ice."

"For a world-class sleuth, you seem to be missing an obvious hole in your theory. Why would I be paying you to find the killer if I am the killer? By the way, am I the shooter or the poisoner? Do you know what I think? I think you like to pour a little brandy in the punch bowl, stir it around, and see what mischief comes of it. What do you say we get down to the real suspects? Give them to me from most likely to least likely"

Give the devil her due, she was damn good. She was paying me, so I figured she was entitled to my opinion.

"The primary suspect is Senior, the target of the shakedown. Next is Junior; he's a wastrel that Senior was planning to supplant with your partner. Then, there is Mercedes. Maybe she figured out what was going on and decided to get her own revenge."

"That mouse. Don't make me laugh. No other suspects?"

"There's a guy named Teller, society sleuth. He was paid to do the background investigation on your brother. Dresses up the Miller's dirty work in two-hundred-dollar suits and Italian calfskin loafers. I think he let his secretary handle the background check and cashed the check. That's exactly the way a bait and cover is supposed to work, isn't it?"

"My, but you are smarter than you look. You even have the trade talk down. Let me guess. Teller is a suspect because if word gets around he blew the background check, he'll be finished with the well-heeled crowd. He'll have to drop down to the minor leagues with you. No offense."

"None taken. He'll have to get used to working with clients like you."

"Speaking of which," she said, "you've got two more days then you're fired."

Chapter 24

Picker, Roz, and I were eating Chinese take-out and sipping Coca-Cola at the office a few hours later. I briefed them on my meetings with Newton and Anne. When she finished, Roz put down her chopsticks and wiped her mouth with a paper napkin.

"Why do you think she fired you?" she asked.

"I'm not fired yet."

"You won't be able to say that two days from now."

"Maybe she didn't like being a suspect," I said.

"Or she's got everything she needs," said Roz.

"Either way, she plans to be done with this and out of here before then," said Picker.

"How do you know that?" asked Roz.

"Once Lou is fired, he is under no obligation to protect her. He can go straight to the cops."

"Like he should have from the beginning."

I forked out another portion of fried rice and Kung Pao chicken. I hadn't mastered chopsticks and had no intention of trying. The Coca-Cola was sticky sweet but went well with the meal. Everyone was mulling over their theories. Picker broke the silence.

"So, there once was a guy. He's part of a confidence team that shakes down rich families. Something goes wrong, and he manages to get himself killed twice. That's got be some kind of record right there. One murder weapon, the rifle, is no problem. You can get one anywhere. It's the second one, the arsenic, that's interesting."

"It's not exactly rare," I said.

"True. You can get it at a pharmacy, hardware store, or a dozen other places, but how can you get it without leaving a paper trail or running the risk of someone picking you out of a lineup?"

"You could ask a shyster like Teller if he has a guy that can help."

"No good. That drags other people into the conspiracy which means more potential witnesses."

"So, what are you saying? We're looking for someone who just happened to have a bottle of arsenic lying around."

"How about a couple of vats of the stuff?" said Picker.

"Boys, slow down a minute. You're moving too fast for me," protested Roz.

"I'm not following either," I said.

"This may come as a surprise to you, but I wasn't always the suave man-about-town you see before you. I dropped out of school when I was fifteen and took any work I could to earn a meal and keep a roof over my head. One of those jobs was in construction. You ever hear of pressure-treated wood?"

"Heard the term, but don't what it is," I said.

"It's wood that's been treated against rot and insects. Do you know what they treat it with? Arsenic."

"Then the Millers," I said, "would have access to large quantities of the stuff, and a small amount needed to poison a man would never be missed. Are there other substances that can be used to treat wood?"

"Yes," he replied, "but arsenic is the cheapest and most effective."

"How can we confirm they're using arsenic? We can't just ask them; it would warn them we're on their trail."

"There would be invoices from the supplier," said Roz, but they'd be secured in their business office."

"*Secured* is subject to interpretation," said Picker with a grin while grabbing his hat and overcoat. "I gotta see a man about a dog. I'll be in touch. Thanks for dinner."

Roz and I cleaned up the dinner mess and headed out the front door. Visions of a nightcap and scratching Marlowe behind the ears was just what the doctor ordered.

The night air was cool and freshly scrubbed from the rain. The city felt unusually clean. The clouds had scattered revealing a full moon that reflected off the wet hood of the Merc. I put Roz in the passenger seat and moved around to the driver's side. The first shot rang out as I cleared the grille and stepped out on to the street. It shattered the driver's-side rearview mirror, sending splinters of glass flying. I hit the deck and yelled for Roz to stay down.

I crawled under the car as the second shot pierced the left front tire. I reached tor my gun and remembered I wasn't carrying one. I tried to get a look at the shooter, but as a third shot bounced off the asphalt, I reflexively covered my head to protect myself from the shell fragments. I peeked out in time to see a shadowy figure carrying a rifle emerge from a doorway across the street, run down the sidewalk, and turn into an alley. I crawled out from under the car and got to my feet. I thought about pursuit, but it was too late for that. Besides, my assailant was armed, and I wasn't. I might be a fool, but I wasn't a damn fool.

"You all right, boss?" asked Roz.

"I'm okay. That's more than I can say for the Merc. How about you?"

"Better than the Merc. Thanks for your concern."

She wanted to be angry, but even in the moonlight, I could see her cheeks were flushed with excitement. She was enjoying this.

"I guess ducking lead is more exciting than filing paperwork," I said.

"Not as eloquent as Churchill," she said, "but you're not wrong."

"Churchill?"

"Nothing in life is so exhilarating as to be shot at and missed," she quoted.

"I don't know about you, but I've had enough exhilaration for one night," I said.

I took off my jacket and rolled up my sleeves. I retrieved the spare and jack from the trunk and tried to change the tire, but my cast was making the task harder than I thought.

"Get out of the way, boss, and let me at that thing," said Roz.

She jacked it up, then bent over and used the tire iron to pop off the hubcap. She put the lug wrench over the first nut, spit on her palms and lifted with all her strength. It gave on the second try. The others came off without protest. She spread my coat on the ground, knelt down, and shimmied the flat off. She replaced it with the spare, lowered the jack, put the tools, hubcap, and flat in the trunk. She stood back, hands on hips, admiring her work.

"Good as new. Can a girl get a ride home?"

"In a minute."

I grabbed a flashlight from under the front seat and walked across the street, heading for the doorway the shots came from. I shone the light on the ground with a specific target in mind. It didn't take long before I saw the gleam of a brass casing. I pulled out a handkerchief and retrieved it, a .22 caliber. Not much firepower for a professional hitman. I found the other two casings in short order, put them in my pocket, returned to the car, and drove away.

When we got to her building, I pulled up to the curb and started to get out. I planned to walk her to her door and see her safely inside, but before I could, she put her hand on my right forearm.

"Hold on a minute, Lou."

I could tell she wanted to talk, so I tapped out a couple of *Camels* and lit them both. She sat puffing while searching for the right words. I wondered if my irresistible charm had finally worked its magic. Her eyes were barely visible in the darkness but seemed illuminated by some internal fire. She was smiling.

"Lou," she began, "about tonight…"

"I'm sorry, Roz. I shouldn't have let my guard down. You were in danger."

"Shut up, you big lug. I'm not sore. I had the best time. I want to make sure you know that before you run off feeling guilty about putting the little lady in jeopardy. All I've wanted my whole life was a taste of excitement, to step out of the dreary and ordinary existence most of us are condemned to…to feel alive. Thanks to you, I got a taste of that tonight, and I want more. Thanks for letting me be part of this investigation. Oh, one other thing. I'm going to continue giving you grief when I think you're fouling up. Bill Newton comes to mind and, of course, your drinking. One of these days, I'm going to get my P.I. ticket, and if we're going to be partners, you need to shape up. *Rizzo and Ellison, Private Investigators.* That's got a nice ring to it. Have a good night. I'll see you in the morning or whenever you show up."

I waited at the curb while my future business partner unlocked the front door and disappeared inside. So much for my irresistible charm. It was better this way.

Chapter 25

Marlowe met me at the front door. I couldn't tell if he was glad to see me or was anticipating dinner. His first priority was to run out in the yard and take care of business. I waited for him at the door. When he got back, I told him to sit, then gave him the third degree.

"Did you earn your keep today?"

He wagged his tail which I took to be a yes.

"Someone just tried to kill me. You notice anything suspicious around here?"

He wagged his tail again which I took as a no. I stepped inside and switched on the light. I gave the place the once over just to ease my mind. Marlowe never lied to me, but there was no point in taking chances. I was tired and needed sleep, but first I needed to call Bill Newton. It was 11 PM. I'd probably be waking him, but as a cop, he was used to it. His wife answered on the second ring and handed me off to Bill.

"Lou, it's eleven, can't it wait until morning?"

"Somebody tried to kill me an hour ago."

"Did he have any luck?"

"Funny."

"Okay. How and where?"

"Three shots from a .22 caliber rifle on the street in front of my office. Roz was with me?"

"Anyone hurt?"

"No, but my Mercury received some flesh wounds."

"Did you get a look at the guy?

"Just a shadow beating it out of there after the fireworks. I recovered three .22 casings. I did it nice and neat, so prints should be fine."

"Pretty lightweight stuff, more suitable for plugging small game than big-shot private eyes. You at home now?"

"Yeah."

"I'll send a couple of uniforms over to retrieve the casings. I'll also have them keep an eye on your place tonight. Can't lose the world's greatest sleuth on my watch."

There was no point going to bed until the cops arrived. I decided to pour myself a shot of courage to calm my nerves. Before I did, I retrieved the pistol from my nightstand and made sure it was loaded. I settled in my wing chair with Marlowe curled up at my feet. I knocked back a whiskey in one swallow and placed the empty on the end table next to the pistol. I don't know how long I sat there lost in thought before I was dragged back to reality by a persistent knocking at the door. I looked down at Marlowe who was resting peaceably.

"Fine watchdog you are," I remarked, earning me another wag.

I grabbed my gun, cracked the front door without unlatching, and peered out. There were two uniforms, a tall, slender sergeant, and a shorter patrolman standing there.

"You gonna let us in or not?" asked the sergeant.

"How do I know you're legit?"

"Lieutenant Newton sent us over to pick up some shell casings and to babysit you tonight. Now, how would we know that if we weren't on the level?"

That made sense. I unlatched the door, and they stepped in.

"Would you mind pointing that peashooter somewhere else?" asked the sergeant.

"Sorry, can't be too careful. Somebody tried to perforate me a couple of hours ago."

"We heard about that. Any description of the guy we should be looking for?"

"I only saw him in the shadows, but he appeared to be short. About the size of your partner." *Or the guy that fractured my fingers in the diner*, I thought.

"I'm tall enough to take care of you," said the patrolman.

Guys like that always felt like they had something to.prove. I let it ride.

I handed the casings, still wrapped in my handkerchief, to the sergeant, thanked them for keeping an eye on the place, and shuffled off to bed.

I didn't get much sleep. Instead, I tossed and turned trying to put the pieces of the Jansen puzzle together. I also had a new problem. Whoever sent me the message to drop the case had upped the ante. Tonight was no warning; it had deadly intent.

Chapter 26

Roz and Picker were engaged in conversation when I managed to drag myself into the office. Roz was leaning in closer than necessary. If Picker took any notice, he gave no indication. He smiled at me and shook his head.

"Roz tells me I left a few minutes too early and missed all the excitement. You certainly got under somebody's skin."

"Hard to believe, as charming as he is," added Roz.

"Have you seen the *Globe-Democrat* today?" he asked.

"No, haven't had time."

Roz handed me a copy. The headline was sensational.

DOUBLE DEAD, it screamed in bold type. It was followed by an article under a new byline. The society page editor had been bounced back to chaperoning the style section.

In a startling turn of events, a reliable source has confirmed to this reporter that Victor Jansen, shot at the altar on his wedding day, was also poisoned. The official autopsy reports that a lethal dosage of arsenic was found in the victim's body. Lieutenant William Newton, the detective in charge of the case, was unavailable for comment. There has been no reported progress in the investigation and my sources at city hall say the mayor is close to removing Newton from the case. The questions John Q. Public wants answered are who was Victor Jansen and who murdered him twice? The mayor is ultimately responsible for public safety and his success, or lack thereof, in this matter will surely not go unnoticed by the voting public.

The rest was just column filler. I ran my fingers through my hair and let out a low whistle. Things were going to get even more uncomfortable for Lieutenant Bill Newton, and my lack of candor was making matters worse. A friend deserved better. Picker sensed my discomfort and changed the subject.

"I'm making a run at Miller's Lumber tonight."

"Say that again."

"I said I'm making a run at Miller's tonight."

"Operation that big must have a night shift. Be swarming with people," I said.

"Roz made a phone call."

"I made a couple," she said, "I needed to be certain."

"I posed as a secretary for an office supply salesman who wanted to make a call on the office manager at 5:30 PM. I was told that was impossible. The office and factory closed at 6 PM, sharp and at 6:01 it was a ghost town. She explained business had been a little slow, so they had to temporarily layoff the graveyard shift. I thanked her and made an appointment for the following day. She gave me directions to the office. It's on an elevated platform that overlooks the factory floor. The only access is via a grated stairway, three flights, and two landings."

"It's in plain view; we'll never make it."

"We?" said Picker.

"Yeah. I'm going with you."

"You looking to add breaking and entering to your resume? Do you think I can't find an invoice? What about Newton's orders you stay away?" he asked.

"He said to steer clear of the Millers, not their office. Besides, three eyes are better than two. Doesn't matter. As I said, it's impossible."

"Lou," said Picker, "you disappoint me. While you two were playing cops and robbers last night, I was casing the place. They're doing security on the cheap. There's a guard at the front gate who records comings and goings and a solitary night watchman who patrols both the grounds and the factory. If you're set on coming, meet me here at midnight, wear something dark, and try not to get yourself killed before then."

He rose, winked at Roz, and left.

"That's a dreamy hunk of man," said Roz wistfully. "What's our next move?"

"We're going to the precinct and give Newton a report on last night's shooting. He'll want to talk to both of us. Grab your coat and let's go."

The desk sergeant announced us and motioned us back to Bill's office. He rose when Roz entered and introduced a second, younger man with a muscular frame, dark hair, and serious demeanor as Detective Dominic Gallo. He invited us to sit. Since there were only two available chairs, Gallo leaned against the wall to the left of Newton's desk.

"I'd like to review the shooting incident from the beginning for Detective Gallo's benefit. Lou, why don't you take the narrative and Miss Ellison can jump in at any time to add or correct the story."

"Roz and I had just finished a meeting in my office."

"With who?" interrupted Newton.

"Whom," corrected Roz. Then, "Sorry, Lieutenant sometimes I can't help myself."

"College girl?"

"Guilty."

"It's all right. Reminds me of my eldest. I'm used to the idiot treatment. Gallo," he said to the younger man, "steer clear of college girls. They're not worth the trouble."

"We were with a client," I said.

"A client. Is that correct, Miss Ellison?"

"Yes, it is. A jealous husband, suspicious of his wife."

"All right. Continue."

"It was around 8 PM when we left the office..."

"Working late," interrupted Newton again. "You two must have been starving."

"We ate Chinese at my desk. I picked it up at the joint around the corner from my office. Roz usually catches a bus or walks home after work, but given the hour, I insisted on driving her home. I put her in the passenger seat which was on the office side of the street. I went around the front grille to the driver's door which was on the street side."

"Did you see anyone? Were there any cars on the road?"

"No, nothing. As soon as I came around to the driver's side the first shot rang out. It blasted my rearview mirror which was between me and the door. A second shot hit the left front tire which was behind me. I dove under the car for cover. There's a red Merc parked in front of the precinct with a shattered mirror and a tire with a bullet hole in the trunk. You can't miss it."

"What did you do, Miss Ellison?"

"I flattened out on the front seat and opened the glove box looking for a pistol."

"You keep a heater in your glove box, Rizzo?" asked Newton.

"No."

"Now he tells me," said Roz. "All the private dicks in the movies do."

"What happened next?"

"I looked around but couldn't see anybody. A third shot hit the asphalt about three feet in front of me. The next one probably would have gotten me, but the shooter lost his nerve and bolted. That's when I got my only look at him, short in stature with longish hair. He was carrying a rifle. Could have been the same guy who mashed my hand, but that's just a guess. I couldn't identify him. I only saw him from behind as he was running away."

"Why didn't you go back to your office and call the cops?"

"It would have been the smart thing to do," I agreed.

"Which is why you didn't do it."

If this kept up much longer, I was going to get my feelings hurt. I finished the narrative.

"I figured there might be shell casings, so I grabbed a flashlight from the beneath the seat and searched the doorway where I had seen my assailant flee. Sure enough, I found all three. I handled them carefully and surrendered them to your men last night."

"You disturbed a crime scene, impeding an investigation."

"Were there any prints?"

"Wiped clean."

"Criminals are getting pretty savvy these days," I said. "There was nothing else to do, so I changed the tire and headed home."

"Is that about right, Miss Ellison?"

"No, it's not," she said.

Newton and Gallo both leaned in.

"I changed the tire."

"Chivalry is dead," said Newton.

"Any other questions?" I asked.

"Just one," said Detective Gallo. "Who's your mysterious client with an interest in this case?"

"You know I can't tell you that."

"Look, paisan, I don't want any of your dago double-speak. Your office isn't a confessional, and you're sure-as-hell no priest. How about you drop that omerta jazz and come clean with us."

"For God's sake, Lou. Tell them the truth," blurted Roz. "If you don't I will."

I wondered what the hell she was doing. I'd have to teach her *Rizzo's First Law of Police Interrogation: Shut up and deny everything.*

Bill sat with his elbows on his desk and fingers steepled while Gallo stood with his arms crossed. They waited expectantly, knowing they had me. They were in no rush.

"Her name is Anne Purcell, and she claims to be the victim's sister. I'll save you some time; she's registered at the Mayfair."

"Purcell? I thought the name was Jansen," said Gallo.

"We suspect they also operated as a husband and wife team in Dallas. They went by Charles and Donna Morgan. I've already told you about that."

"And what exactly is she paying you to do?" asked Bill.

"Find her brother's killer before you do."

"I can't wait to hear why she'd want to that," he said.

"She says she wants to dispense justice herself."

"If she's successful, that will make you an accessory to murder," said Gallo. "We've already got you on withholding evidence in a homicide. You can kiss your P.I. ticket goodbye."

"Everybody calm down," said Bill. "Detective Gallo and Miss Ellison, if you'll excuse us for a moment, I have some things I need to discuss with Mr. Rizzo."

After Roz and Gallo made their exit, Bill leveled a steady gaze on me.

"I don't know where to begin, Lou. You knew I was at a dead end with this investigation, and the villagers were at the castle door with torches and pitchforks. Yet, you chose to sit on the best lead we have in this case. I don't give two shakes about my career; it ain't worth a bucket of spit anyway, but as a matter of personal pride, I'd sure like to crack this thing. Shut the brass up. Why'd you hold out on me?"

"Bill, Anne Purcell is a slick customer. If she got even a sniff that you were on her tail, she'd be in the wind, and this murder would never be solved. I figure her revenge story for pure hogwash. She's a confidence woman who is still trying to get a payout. She'll hang on to that bone until it becomes too risky. She knows something, but not everything. She needs to find a connection between the killer and the mark, so she can extort him. That's what she's hired me to do. The revenge story is just a cover for her real motive."

"So, you are trying to out-con a con woman? Maybe I would have played along if you'd given me a chance. Now that Gallo knows about her, we need to pick her up. Do you understand what I'm telling you?"

I was pretty sure I did.

"Bill, have you had an opportunity to interview the Millers?"

"Only briefly and with their mouthpiece present. They deny any knowledge of a shakedown or foul play. I couldn't lean on them too hard; they have a lot of top cover."

"Have you done any additional background research on them?"

"Gallo has done a lot of legwork. The guy's a pain in the ass, but he's efficient. Patrick Miller, Senior is your typical American success story. He started with nothing and built a nice little business. Made his fortune by buying up his competitors and eventually gaining a stranglehold on the market. If a competitor asked too high a price or was reluctant to sell, he would drop the price on his products and drive them out of business. He realized early on that he would need political cover, so he became a frequent and generous campaign contributor. Bottom line, the guy plays hardball and is accustomed to getting his way."

"Patrick Miller, Junior is cut from a different bolt of cloth. The old man doesn't think much of him and with good cause. He liked the trappings that money and status brought but was disinclined to put any work into earning them. He spent most of his time either at the country club or the many social clubs he belonged to. He likes to gamble and is neither a big winner nor a big loser. He has no major outstanding debts, but he is dependent on the company, where he is the nominal VP, for his finances. Reportedly, he only shows up at the office once or twice a week. It was a nice setup until Jansen came along. The old man fell in love with him and saw him as his replacement when the time came. That was a direct threat to Junior's lifestyle. On the surface, their relationship was cordial, but according to friends, Junior wouldn't shed any tears if Jansen was out of the picture."

"Mercedes was by all accounts, is a spoiled young woman overindulged by her father. She had no further ambitions than to attend finishing school and find a husband. Senior tried unsuccessfully for years to make a match for her with some promising young man who might be capable of taking over the business. With her average looks and vapid interests, she couldn't compete with her peers. The family had almost given up hope when Jansen came riding in on a white charger to rescue her."

"That's about all we know. Senior and Junior look like viable suspects. Mercedes acts like she just landed from Mars. She's an odd young woman. Not a viable suspect in Gallo's opinion."

I thanked Bill for the update and started to leave, promising to do a better job keeping him in the loop.

"Don't forget what I told you before," he said.

We left it at that.

Chapter 27

Roz was waiting for me outside the precinct. She was working on a smoke.

"Nice job covering for Picker, Roz. Wish you had done the same for me."

"It was time to come clean and save your hide while you still could," she replied. "I was saving you from yourself."

"I'll buy you lunch to show my gratitude."

"I can't. I have an appointment in an hour."

"Business-related; I trust."

"Absolutely."

"Where can I drop you off."

"Riverfront Christian."

"What are you up to?"

"Applying for a job as choir director. You might have heard, there's an opening."

"What do you hope to find out?"

"Who knows. It's quite a coincidence that Clayborn got fired within days of the murder. Maybe someone knows more than they're saying. Maybe some of the good Christian ladies on the staff have loose tongues."

There was a phone booth next to where I'd parked the Merc. I had a call to make before we went anywhere. I told Roz I'd be right with her, pointed her towards the car, and slid into the booth. I dropped a nickel into the slot and dialed the Mayfair.

"What was that all about?" asked Roz when I got behind the wheel.

"Nothing."

I dropped Roz in front of the church and headed back to the office. I grabbed an egg salad sandwich at Nestor's and carried it back to my desk. Before I could manage to take a bite, there was a knock. I was expecting a visitor, but not so soon. Halfway to the door, I turned back, pulled a pistol from my desk drawer, and tucked it in my belt. I opened the door.

Standing there was the goon who busted my hand. I whipped my gun out and aimed at his chest. He put his hands up to demonstrate he was no threat. He had lost the smug look he displayed in the diner and replaced it with a more contrite one. I wasn't taking any chances. I kept my rod pointed at his chest.

"You got another message for me?"

"No, but I have some dope for you. Can I put my hands down?"

"Pull your jacket back. I need to frisk you."

He complied, and I patted him down. He was clean. I motioned him to sit. He removed his hat and fiddled nervously with the brim. Beads of perspiration were forming on his lip. I had no idea I was so intimidating.

"Are you going to sit there and squirm like a kid caught with his hand in the cookie jar, or are you going to say what you came here to say?"

"You want to know who hired me to shut you up?"

"Yeah."

"It was that shyster, Teller."

"Why."

"I ain't his advisor. I'm just an employee. You know how it is. If he needs someone to fix the sink, he calls a plumber. If he needs someone to fix a light switch, he calls an electrician. If he needs some muscle, he calls me. He just gives me a name and tells me what to do. In your case, it was to deliver a warning."

I showed him my cast.

"This was bad enough but shooting at me is over the line."

"Look, I'll cop to the hand, but I don't know anything about a shooting. I'm taking a risk talking to you. If this gets out, I'm going to be getting fitted for a pair of concrete brogans. You're not going to the cops, are you? Might as well take a contract out on me."

I just let that hang in the air. Let the weasel sweat.

"What's your name?" I asked.

"Joe Kowalczyk, it's Polish for blacksmith. That's what they call me on the streets, the Blacksmith."

"What brought you here today. Your conscience keeping you up at nights? Fall off your ass on the road to Damascus?"

"Can't afford a conscience in my business; been knocked on my ass a few times. Where the hell is Damascus anyway? Illinois? I'm here because I had a visitor last night. While I was sleeping, I got a creepy feeling that someone was watching me. When I opened my eyes there was this tall guy at the foot of my bed. He wore a snazzy suit and looked more like one of those society types than an enforcer. He was tapping the barrel of a Louisville slugger and smiling. Not one of those glad-to-see-you smiles, but one that said he was going to enjoy rearranging my face. Gave me the willies. We had a one-sided conversation. He talked, I listened. He made an impression That's all I'm gonna say. I gave you what you wanted. Tell your friend we're even."

I got up from my chair and walked over to him. I put my cast on his shoulder and smiled. With my other hand, I drove the grip of my pistol into the side of his face. I heard the satisfying sound of bones crunching and saw blood spurting from his mouth and nose. He fell to the floor and curled up in the fetal position. I grabbed him by the hair, pulled him to his feet, slapped his hat on his head, and pushed him out into the hall.

"Now we're even," I called after him. "Come back when you're feeling better. You left a couple of teeth on the floor."

There was little doubt who put the fear of God in the Blacksmith. I wondered how Picker found him and what he said to convince such a hard case to pay me a visit and rat out his employer. I'd probably never know.

Chapter 28

I took off my jacket, rolled up my sleeves, and went to work cleaning the blood off the floor. I was on my hands and knees, towel in hand when the door swung open and Anne walked in. She was wearing a dark suit with an expensive silk blouse tied in a bow below the neck. She looked good but that was nothing new. She took in the scene without comment.

"Where's that dreadful secretary of yours?"

"Running errands."

"What happened here?"

"There was a little accident," I said.

"I can see that. What I don't see is where you're bleeding from, so I assume someone else had the accident. That's none of my concern. Your message said the cops had my scent. How'd they get it if you didn't tell them?"

"I have no idea. Someone tried to kill me last night. Three shots, all near misses. I laid the next part on thick. The cops gave me the bare lightbulb treatment, sweated me pretty hard. They claimed they knew I had a client with an interest in the Jansen murder case, and the attempt on my life was probably related."

"Who would know about your mystery client besides you?" she said giving me a suspicious look.

She didn't deserve the truth, so I didn't give it to her.

"Teller," I said. "I had to tell him why I was poking around the case. He must have told the cops."

"The society dick?"

"Yup."

"That was careless on your part," she said. "I suppose it's possible. Let's say it is. What do we do next?"

"I think I'm close to solving the case. I should have an answer for you in the morning. In the meantime, we need to find a place to stash you. I suggest my place. No one will look for you there. Where are your bags?"

"I left them at the office door."

"Good, we'll grab them on the way out. Let's go."

Once I had her in the car, she was a captive audience, giving me the chance to ask a few questions.

"When was the last time you saw your brother?"

"About a month ago."

"You want me to believe your brother double-crossed you, and you've been sitting idly by for a month. Give me some credit, doll."

"Who said he double-crossed me?"

"You spend months setting up your con, and he decides to marry the mark, cutting you out of the payoff and leaving himself sitting pretty. If that's not a double-cross, what do you call it?"

"Okay, there was some bad blood at first, but we got past it."

"But it wasn't a month ago, was it?"

"No. We had breakfast on the day of the wedding. We reconciled, I wished him well and made myself scarce. I was planning on leaving the next day and moving on to the next caper. That all changed when some mope drilled him. Now, as I've already told you, I'm in it for revenge."

"Was he your brother, husband, lover, or just a partner?"

"Depends on which city and which caper we were working. What difference does it make?"

"None, forget I asked."

We rode in silence for a while until she asked, "This Teller guy, is he a short brutish guy with a cauliflower ear?"

"No, but he's got someone like that working for him."

That was the end of the conversation. I rolled up in front of my house, parked and we went in. Marlowe greeted us warmly. He was a sucker for a good-looking dame. It was a weakness he'd need to overcome if he wanted to become a big-time sleuth. I should know. She shooed him away with the outside of her foot which was a major strike against her in my book. *Rizzo's First Law of Character Analysis: Any woman who doesn't like dogs can't be trusted.* Marlowe, gentle soul that he is, would forgive her, but I wouldn't. I grabbed her bags from the trunk and hauled them into the bedroom.

"You sleep in here," I said, "and I'll take the couch. There are clean sheets in the closet and spare towels in the bath. I have to be somewhere tonight. It might take a while so don't wait up for me. There's some leftover chicken in the fridge and some spirits in the cabinet to the right. Marlowe will tell you what he needs. His food is under the sink."

"You said you expected to crack the case tonight," she said. "What makes you so certain?"

"I've got all the pieces I need but am lacking a final bit of evidence. I hope to lay my hands on that tonight. If so, I can wrap this thing up and put a nice big bow on it."

Anne excused herself to freshen up and I opened the bottom drawer of my dresser and pulled out a dark sweater, a wool cap, and a pair of gloves. I hoped that was what the fashionable thief was wearing this season. I put a few other things in order and prepared to leave. When Anne returned, I put my hand under Marlowe's muzzle and stared into his eye.

"Keep a sharp lookout when I'm gone. She's your responsibility."

I turned to Anne.

"You'll be safe here. Marlowe's a good watchdog." He wagged his tail, pleased by the glowing endorsement. "If you need it, there's a pistol in the nightstand next to the bed."

Chapter 29

I had changed clothes in the office and met Picker at the appointed time. He surveyed me critically, adjusted my wool cap, and stepped back.

"Now you look like a proper cat-burglar."

We briefly went over the plan for the evening. Picker reviewed the details. He cased the joint the night before. It was, as Roz had reported, deserted after 6 PM. The exception being a security guard at the front gate and a night watchman who roamed the grounds. The gate guard didn't figure to be a problem; we'd make our entrance through the delivery gate which was locked but unattended. The night watchman was another matter. No telling where he'd be. We'd need to keep a sharp eye out for him. Picker suggested a 2 AM approach. By then, both security guys would be a little dull around the edges.

That gave us about an hour to kill. I suggested a drink to steady our nerves, but Picker waved it off.

"Not while I'm working. Got to stay sharp. I suggest we get to Miller's thirty minutes early and get a feel for the situation. Things can change from night to night. Our biggest enemy is the unexpected."

We left the office, got in the Merc, and headed toward the factory. The drive was a rare opportunity to be alone with Picker. I knew him to be a very private man, not inclined to share any details about his life. He proved on many occasions to be a loyal friend. I often wondered if I was the only one he had. Not counting the other night, we never shared a meal or even a drink outside my office. He was a phantom, going about his business, then melting into his surroundings. Considering his elegant appearance, how he managed was a total mystery. I wondered if he shared any details with Roz during one of their office chats. Not likely. He had an arsenal of skills that set him apart from the common thief. Where had he learned his trade?

I made it a point to respect his privacy. It was a key element in our friendship. Maybe it was the apprehension I was feeling about tonight's break-in, but I decided to take a flyer.

"How does someone become Picker?" I asked trying not to sound too intrusive.

I was surprised by his response.

"You've always done a good job allowing me to be your friend without meddling in my personal affairs.

Not many guys, especially in your line of work, can contain their curiosity as long as you have."

"It hasn't been easy," I said. "Reminds me of my B-25 days. Imagine trying to decode your target coordinates without the codebook. I don't have the book on you. The real enigma is how you learned to do what you do."

"What is it you think I do?"

"You portray yourself as a small-time thief, but I think you're more than that. I know from experience you have impressive powers of persuasion with even the hardest of hard cases. That's amazing all by itself since I've never even seen you sore. You can menace without violence. You're a skilled forger, pickpocket, and safecracker. You never get flustered. I'm sweating bullets in anticipation of what we're going to do tonight while you look as cool as a cucumber. And of course, you have something the dames can't resist. Look at poor Roz."

"She's a good egg. Hang on to her, Lou."

"I intend to, but you haven't answered the question. How did you learn to be Picker?"

He gave that some thought before answering.

"Who I am or rather who I was in my previous life isn't important. The skills you mention can be leaned by any punk on the street. The trick is to be the best at it. That takes more time than they are willing to invest. They won't put in the work to improve their craft. They'd rather be drinking, gambling or skirt-chasing. In the long run, that attitude lands most of them in the slammer."

"I suppose if I applied the same approach in any field, I could have been a success, but I would have been unhappy. The machine would have swallowed me up as it does with most. I like my life. I like my freedom and, best of all, I like the thrill I feel when the game is afoot. You know what I'm talking about. It's the reason you became a P.I., even if it was your second choice. I never take too much, only what I need. I'm like Robin Hood, except I don't give to the poor."

"How do you learn to intimidate the bad guys and charm the ladies?" he continued. "It's two sides to the same coin. You have to become a student of human nature which means you need to be observant. I've learned more about what makes people tick by eavesdropping on adjoining tables when I dine or spending an afternoon at Union Station or Forrest Park. Most men are cowards at heart. Figure out their fears and exploit them. Most women want three things:

a man who will listen, a little flattery for her self-esteem, and someone who can make her laugh."

When we were within about a quarter mile of our destination, Picker told me to pull over. I didn't know any more about him than before, which I suspect was his plan.

"We'll walk from here," he said. "We don't want some bum to stumble across your car and ID it to the cops. If all goes well, they'll never know we were here, but discretion is still the better part of valor."

We walked in silence with Picker leading the way. When we were across the street from the service gate, he went to one knee and motioned me to do the same. From our position, we could make out the light coming from inside the guard shack at the main entrance. It was unlikely the gate guard would be able to spot us from there. That left the night watchman to worry about. The factory was ringed with a series of pole-mounted spotlights about fifty yards apart bathing it in a soft glow. One was mounted next to the loading dock which was where we planned to enter the building. We'd be easy to spot if he happened to be patrolling that way.

Both of us were unarmed. He liked to say he survived by wits, not savagery. Someone could always muster more firepower, but few could outsmart him.

Clouds obscured the sky, blocking out any moonlight. A bolt of lightning lit up the entire scene and was followed by the rumble of thunder. The air smelled like rain and electricity. It wasn't long before I felt a drop, then another. Suddenly, it was pouring. Picker got to his feet and motioned me toward the service gate. He spoke in hushed tones.

"This should drive the watchman indoors and give us a clear shot at the service gate and loading dock entrance."

We made our way to the gate, which was fastened with a heavy chain and padlock. Picker made short work of the lock and we let out just enough slack in the chain to allow us to squeeze through. He rearranged everything to look like nothing had been disturbed but left the lock open in case we had to scram in a hurry.

When we felt certain the coast was clear, we sprinted down the short service road to the dock. The door to the interior was locked, but it was child's play for Picker. Once again, we squeezed through the smallest opening that would allow our passage. Picker closed the door and locked it. I gave him a quizzical look and he pointed to a small rectangular box mounted on the wall. It was hinged on one side and needed a key to open it. It was a watch box that would record the security guard's presence after he inserted his key and turned it. They were placed at strategic locations and prevented a watchman from sleeping on his shift. If he missed a station on his scheduled route, his superiors would know about it the next day. The guard was nowhere to be seen, so he must have been somewhere else in the building.

The interior was illuminated by a series of overhead lamps. Every fifth light was burning. The others were presumably turned on during business hours. We were standing in the warehouse, one of two large rooms. The other was the factory with the milling equipment. That was the room where the office was located on the second story grating. We made our way cautiously from one stack of lumber to the next, the sweet smell of freshly cut wood flooding our nostrils.

Picker grabbed a shop-rag lying on a bundle of lumber. He wiped the soles of his shoes and tossed me the towel. I did the same. We didn't want to leave a trail of watery footprints.

We crossed the length of the warehouse and were standing at the entry to the factory when we saw a flashlight beam panning over the area we recently vacated. A short, older man in a security guard's uniform was making his rounds. He was moving away from us, so we entered the factory and looked up at the grating that surrounded the ground floor. An austere looking office with windows facing the factory was visible where we expected it. We headed for the stairs. The damp leather soles of our shoes made barely audible squishes, but they sounded like Count Basie's brass section to me.

We got to the base of the stairs, where Picker pointed out another watch box. That made sense but added to my anxiety. He motioned us up the stairs. They creaked as we ascended. We made it to the first landing, a third of the way up, when we saw the flashlight beam approaching. Picker flattened himself against the grate, and I did the same. The beam worked its way up the stairs passing over our heads and shone on the office, then it switched off. We heard the watch box open and close, followed by the sounds of footsteps walking away. Picker smiled and motioned up the stairs. He was in his element and enjoying himself.

Another door, another lock, and we were in the office. I told Picker to keep an eye out for the watchman while I went through the files.

"Fine, but keep your flashlight aimed below the window line."

We taped over most of the lens, leaving only a small slot for a beam. That was standard procedure for convoy headlights during the war. I found the filing cabinets and began my search. In the top drawer of the second cabinet, there was a file labeled invoices and I started working through the documents. It would have been an easy task if I knew the name of the vendor, everything was filed alphabetically. I finally found what I was looking for. Three, 200-pound drums of chromated copper arsenate shipped from Brunson Chemicals. They would have a record of the sale, meaning I wouldn't need this invoice. As fruit of the poisonous tree, it would be worthless in court anyway.

Picker gave me a thumbs-up for all clear.

"Get what you needed?"

"Yes, let's get out of here."

"In a minute. My curiosity is killing me," he said pointing to a medium-sized rectangular safe in the far corner. "I wonder what's in there?"

"Nothing of use to us," I said.

"How do you know unless we look? It's a '44 Defender. I've never cracked one of those. I have to give it a try. It would be unprofessional not to. It's got a standard three-wheel lock. Shouldn't be much of a problem. You stand lookout while I give this baby a whirl."

He removed his gloves and stuck them in his hip pocket. Kneeling in front of the safe, he laid his flashlight on the floor and put his ear to the side of the dial. He rotated the dial clockwise to clear the tumblers. His face was a study in concentration. He then slowly turned it counterclockwise and leaned back. The dim light from his flashlight revealed small beads of perspiration on his forehead. He leaned back in and repeated the process. This time, there was a satisfied grin on his face.

He slowly moved the dial to the right. That produced another grin. A subsequent rotation to the left brought a triumphant smile. He grabbed the lever and pulled. The door swung open. He aimed his flashlight inside and extracted the only contents of the safe, a manilla envelope. It contained two banded stacks of one-hundred-dollar bills and two business envelopes. He handed me the envelopes while he thumbed each stack of cash like a card-shark counting a new deck.

"Ten grand," was all he said.

Both letters were addressed to Patrick Miller, Sr. and marked *Personal and confidential.* Neither had a return address, but both were postmarked St. Louis. One was dated two weeks before the wedding, the other three days prior. I opened the first. It was typed and unsigned. *Victor Jansen is a fraud. Will provide proof for twenty thousand dollars. Place add in Globe personals stating "Miss you, Joan" to confirm.* The second letter read; *I can solve your problem for ten thousand dollars. Have a man meet me at Union Station on the benches across from the ticket counter. Have him wear a red carnation in his lapel.*

I passed the letters to Picker who read them and said, "Your client attempted to double-cross her double-crossing partner by under-bidding him, but she was asking too much. As the wedding got closer, she got nervous and reduced the price. She also crossed some invisible line. She was prepared to commit murder, which is highly unusual for a confidence man or woman. Smells of desperation. A real professional," he said with contempt, "would have eaten her losses and walked away. She gives the rest of us a bad name."

"Picker, you're a thief for god-sakes."

"You disappoint me, Lou. I have my standards."

"I meant no offense. Can we sort this out later? Let's get out of here pronto," I said.

"What about the money and the letters?"

"Leave them. If anything turns up missing, Miller will know someone's been here. If we take it, none of it can be used in court. Besides, we don't want to add robbery to our sheet."

Picker smiled.

"Relax, Lou. You know I'm not the type for a big score."

He placed the manilla envelope back in the safe, closed the lever, and spun the dial. Then he took out a handkerchief, wiped the safe clean, and put his gloves back on.

We were about to make our escape when the watchman reappeared. He grabbed a chair from against the wall and pulled it next to the deck of a large band saw. He produced a lunch pail and a magazine and settled in for a meal.

"Damn," I said, "the bugger's on his lunch break. What do we do now?"

"The only thing we can do, wait until he finishes. Remember, he's married to the watch box. He's got a schedule to keep. Might as well make ourselves comfortable."

We both sat on the floor. My back was against the wall, his against the secretary's desk.

"It would be interesting to see a list of those who have the combination to the safe," said Picker.

"Sure would. You got any ideas on how to find out?"

"Maybe you should just ask."

"Maybe I should."

Eventually, the watchman finished his break and left to start his rounds. We seized the opportunity to make our exit. We retraced our route, being careful to put everything back the way it was. I didn't relax until we were in the Merc and headed away from the crime scene. At his request, I dropped Picker off on a street corner and watched as he folded into the night. I headed home.

Chapter 30

Marlowe was waiting for me when I opened the front door. I patted him on the head and let him out. I went to the bedroom to check on Anne. She wasn't there, and the bed had not been slept in. I called to her but got no response. Marlowe let himself back in through the open door.

"Where is she, boy?"

He wagged his tail. As far as he was concerned, all was well. His worries extended no further than his bladder and kibbles. I'd trade lives with him if I could.

"I gave you one job," I reprimanded. "Keep your eye on her, and you turn around and lose her."

He wagged his tail again. He takes criticism well.

I went back to the bedroom. The phone was off the hook, and there was faint dial tone. The handset was tucked under a pillow. She probably used it to call a cab and wanted me to get a busy signal if I tried to phone her. Her bags were still there. I rifled through them looking for each of the four outfits I'd seen her in. The beige suit was missing. My guess was she was wearing it. I opened the drawer on the nightstand; my pistol was missing. Someone was going to have a very bad day.

It was 4 AM. If I was right, nothing was going to happen for another five hours. That gave me time for a quick nap and a shower. I was all but out on my feet and smelled of flop sweat from the break-in. I stripped off my clothes, set the alarm for seven, and collapsed on the bed. I was out before my head hit the pillow.

I was awaked by Marlowe licking my face. I grabbed a hot shower, shaved, and brewed some coffee. It was 8 AM. I called the precinct, left a message for Bill Newton, grabbed my fedora, and drove the Merc to Teller's office building. The elevator took me up to the fifth floor. Teller's door was open, but the place was abandoned. Sarah wasn't at her desk. As usual, I was unarmed. My primary piece was at the office and Anne had my secondary. I needed to rethink that strategy. A brass-handled walking stick stood in a wicker basket by the door. It wasn't much, but it's all I had. I grabbed it and brought it back Stan Musial style.

I called out. "Anybody here? Archie? Sarah?"

Nothing at first, then I heard muffled sounds coming from behind a door to the left of the reception desk. I turned the knob, it was unlocked, and swung it open. Sarah was bound and gagged and seated next to a shelf stocked with supplies. I freed her from her bonds and helped her to her feet. She winced and touched the back of her head where a baseball-sized lump was framed by a sticky blob of semi-dried blood. I managed to get her seated on a couch across from her desk.

"Are you okay?" I asked.

She looked at me like I had the brains of a milk cow.

"Do I look okay?" she groaned.

"Can I get you anything? Some water maybe."

"I think I'm going to be sick."

I dragged a trash can over, and she started retching. While she was occupied, I went to Teller's office. He was leaning back in his chair as if he was listening to a client plead his case. He had two bullet holes in his chest. The desk drawer to his right was half-way open. Inside was a polished Colt .38 Police Special.

I went back to reception and found Sarah had finished emptying her stomach. I've had enough concussions to know that was standard procedure.

"You keep any ice around here?"

She pointed to a small refrigerator next to the supply closet. I put some ice in the scarf used to tie her hands and placed it gently on the back of her head. I took her right hand and placed it over the ice pack.

"What do you remember?" I asked.

"Nothing. I unlocked the office door and woke up in the closet."

Just then, Bill Newton entered accompanied by a pair of uniforms.

"I got your message and got here as quickly as I could. What happened?"

"Someone cold-cocked the secretary and stuck her in the supply closet. Then they paid Archie Teller a visit. He's in his office but won't be seeing visitors. Took two to the chest."

"Archie," screamed Sarah springing to her feet and making for his office.

I grabbed her by the shoulder.

"You don't need to go in there. Bill, can you get one your guys to restrain her?"

He motioned to one of the uniforms. "Take her to the precinct, get a matron, and take her statement."

Chapter 31

Newton entered Teller's office and surveyed the crime scene. One bullet entered mid-sternum; the second was about six inches below that. He observed the open drawer and the pistol.

"Looks like he was reaching for his gun when he was shot," he said.

"That's how I read it."

"We'll pull the slugs and do the ballistics. Might be important if we can recover the murder weapon before it finds its way to the drink."

"I can save you some trouble, it was a .22 Smith & Wesson."

"How do you know that?"

"It was mine."

"You killed Teller?"

"Right. I called you, came here, slugged the secretary from behind so she couldn't ID me, shot Teller, then came back and revived her."

"Don't crack wise with me," snapped Newton. "We're friends, remember? But if you're sure you know the murder weapon, then you must know the killer."

"I do. It was my client."

"Anne Purcell? The woman who mysteriously checked out of the Mayfair after you tipped us?"

"Yeah, that one."

"How'd she get your gun?"

"Stole it from my nightstand."

"You warned her we were coming to pick her up, then you stashed her away at your place. Is that about right?"

"Yup."

"Where were you when she grabbed the gun and bolted?"

"Out collecting evidence."

"You left her unguarded?"

"I told Marlowe to watch her."

"Who's he?"

"My dog."

Bill was working himself into a righteous fury, although he had all but given me permission to spring her from the Mayfair. There was still a second uniform within earshot, so he had to cover his ass at my expense. I had it coming.

"Why'd you do it, Rizzo?" he said shaking his head.

"I needed her in the wind to solve the case."

"You got a guy murdered?"

"That wasn't part of the plan."

"I ought to arrest you right now."

"She's the one who poisoned Jansen."

"She murdered two people...one of them her brother. That's some ruthless dame."

"Technically, she didn't murder Jansen; he died of a bullet wound."

"Did she tell you she poisoned Jansen?"

"Not in so many words, but you can only put a jigsaw puzzle together one way. The pieces must fit. I'll explain it to you later, but if you want to prevent another shooting and put the arm on Anne, we need to get over to Miller's Lumber on the double."

Newton ordered the remaining uniform to guard the door and not let anyone enter until reinforcements arrived. We took the elevator down to street level and got in his cruiser. Using the police radio he called in the Teller murder and ordered backup at the scene. The dispatcher acknowledged the call. He was about to continue by issuing a dragnet for Anne but realized he'd never seen her and had no description.

"What does this dame look like?"

"Tall. About five-eight, thirty-two, maybe thirty-three years old. Red hair, green eyes, fair skin, and statuesque."

"I think I'll leave out the last part. Don't want to attract the interest of the press. They monitor this band. Hopefully, they're all on the Teller scent."

"What is she wearing?"

Can't say for sure, but a beige suit would be a pretty good guess."

He relayed the information to the dispatcher along with a little white lie.

Two minutes later the radio crackled to life.

"Calling all cars. Calling all cars. Be on the lookout for a female, early thirties, five feet eight inches tall, one hundred-twenty-five pounds with red hair, green eyes. Last seen wearing a beige suit. Suspect is wanted for questioning for bank fraud. May be armed. That is all."

"Bank fraud?" I asked.

"Dullest crime in the world and too complicated for the average hack to wrap his brain around. If the ink jockey's monitor the call, they'll ignore it. You gonna tell me why we're going to Miller's."

"Odds are that's where she's headed."

"And how do you know that?"

"Someone paid her to poison Jansen."

"You're saying she's a professional hitman?"

"No. She was Jansen's partner in a con gone wrong. They set the price tag at fifty-grand for Jansen to disappear before the wedding. Jansen screwed things up by falling for the mark. He was still set for life, but she got left holding the bag. First, she tried to warn Miller off by anonymous note. I imagine he went to his daughter who, being in love, dismissed it as malicious gossip. Rather than wasting two months' worth of setup work, Anne offered to solve the problem for a much lower price."

"How much of that fish story is fact and how much is your fertile imagination? Killing your partner seems cold-blooded."

"Since when did you start believing in the goodness of human nature? A man of your experience should have some healthy skepticism by now. To answer your question, Anne told me about the shakedown and her partner's double-cross. She also confessed to having breakfast the morning of the wedding, which was the perfect time to administer the arsenic. The rest is pure guess-work, but it fits."

"Where'd she get arsenic?"

"Miller has barrels of the stuff."

"You sure?"

"Yes, it's used in pressure-treating wood. I've got the name of his supplier."

Why'd she kill Teller?"

"If you step on the gas, we may get to Miller's in time to ask her."

Chapter 32

We arrived at Miller's and approached the guard shack. The guy gave us an open palm indicating we should stop. He approached with a clipboard and asked our business.

"None of yours," snapped Newton displaying his badge. "Which way to the office?"

He gave us directions then added, "I'll call ahead to let them know you're coming."

"You do that, and you will be spending your next shift in the slammer."

He looked at the guy's nametag.

"You read me, Thompson?"

"Yes sir, loud and clear."

"Did you see a redhead in a beige suit come through here?"

"Yes, about ten minutes ago. Came in a cab and asked for office directions too. Said she was here to see Mr. Miller on personal business and wanted to surprise him. Said she'd consider it a personal favor if I didn't call ahead."

"Did she show you any ID?"

"She had a nice smile," he replied sheepishly.

"Did she give you a name for your clipboard?"

"Yes, I forgot about that. It's right here," he said pointing to the last name on the visitor's log. "Norma Mortensen."

Newton drove forward and parked in the vice-president's slot.

"You a movie buff, Lou?"

"Enough of one to know that Marilyn Monroe is apparently visiting Miller as we speak."

We exited the cruiser and headed to the door. We walked in and found ourselves in the factory portion of the building. The place was a beehive of activity with all manner of saws and lathes and planers whirring away. I pointed to the second story office; the shades were drawn, so there was no way of knowing what was going on inside. We followed a painted walk space to the foot of the stairs and began climbing. When we reached the top, Newton drew his police special from its holster.

He grabbed the handle, twisted and we surged into the room. Miller Senior was backed against the wall behind his desk looking down the wrong end of my .22. His secretary was squeezed in a corner trying to make herself look as small as possible. She was shaking like Marlowe in a thunderstorm.

"Hold it right there," he said. "Drop the heater. Now!"

Anne slumped her shoulders in defeat and began to lower the pistol. When Newton relaxed, she raised the gun and fired twice. The secretary screamed. The first shot missed, but the second hit Newton in the shoulder. His gun went skittering across the room as he spun to the floor. I rushed to his assistance. The bullet entered just below the right shoulder. There was no exit wound. The slug was still in there. He was bleeding but not hemorrhaging. No veins had been hit. I plugged the hole with my handkerchief and helped him to a chair.

"Son-of-a-bitch, that hurts."

"It's not too bad. Keep pressure on it to stop the bleeding," I said.

"Rookie mistake," he grumbled. "And with all that racket below us, no one will hear that pop-gun."

"Enough whining, boys," said Anne. "Neither of you move. I've some business to attend to, and then I'll decide what to do with you. Mr. Miller owes me some money; I intend to collect."

"I told you I don't know what you're talking about," growled Miller. It wasn't very convincing. "Why would I owe you money?"

"For services rendered," she said.

"What kind of services?" asked Newton.

"Shut up, quick-draw, or I'll shut you up," she said.

"You see, Bill," I began, "Anne offered to kill her partner for ten-grand, and Miller agreed. It was a bargain for him because the shakedown was for fifty."

"That's nonsense," said Miller. "There was no shakedown."

"Then why did you give Anne the arsenic that was used to poison Jansen?"

"You can't prove I did anything of the sort."

"Teller can," I said.

"He'll never talk," said Miller.

"That's for sure," cracked Anne.

"Maybe the lady will sell you out to make a deal with the DA.

"You're betting on the wrong pony in that race," she said.

"I'll tell you a story, Anne. You stop me when I'm wrong,"

"Why would I do that?" she asked.

"Because at the end of the story. I'll tell you where your money is?"

"All right, I'm listening," she said.

"When your partner, who is neither your brother nor husband, as he was in Dallas, hit you with the double-cross, you swore you were still going to get a payday. You typed an anonymous letter to Miller offering to solve his problem at a discounted rate, but it was still too rich for his blood. When he couldn't convince his daughter to call the wedding off, he started to panic. So, you dropped the price and offered to solve his problem permanently. He's a businessman; that seemed to him like the best deal he was going to get. Twenty cents on the dollar. He agreed, but he needed to be able to deny any involvement, so he went to Teller, who was already in the doghouse for his botched background check."

"Teller also needed deniability, so he hired a street thug named the Blacksmith to meet you at union station and make the deal. You would be paid in full when the problem went away. He also took along a vial of arsenic provided by Miller in case you needed it. You had breakfast with Jansen on the day of the wedding and slipped him the mickey in his coffee. You didn't use enough to kill him immediately because that would shine the light on you, but you gave him enough to kill him within a couple of hours."

"It was a good plan, but you hadn't counted on someone plugging Jansen at the altar. The businessman in Miller decided since you rendered no service, no payment was due. By then, you were in for a dime and in for a dollar and determined to collect. The problem was you didn't know who had the ten grand. You guessed whoever acted as Miller's agent still had the money, but you had no clue who that was. You couldn't be sure it was Senior because you made a foolish mistake and sent an identical letter to Junior. You didn't care which one took the bait as long as you got paid."

"The only person who would know for sure was the guy acting as the agent and you didn't know who that was. That's why you hired me. You didn't give a damn about who shot your partner. You wanted the middleman. You hoped that my investigation would turn over enough rocks to find him. And, like a good little private dick, I did...Teller."

"You went to his office this morning to collect, but he denied having it. You managed to get him to confess Senior was your client. When he tried to get the drop on you, you iced him. A regular Bonnie Parker. There was nothing left for you to do but come directly to Miller and demand your fee. That about right?"

Chapter 33

"That's complete nonsense. You can't prove I ever saw this woman before," said Miller. "You're bluffing."

"Am I?" I replied. "I'll bet that Ten G's is around here somewhere. Maybe even in that safe over there," I said nodding in its direction. "Why don't you open it and we'll have a look?"

Miller's face turned white.

"You need a warrant issued by a judge to look in there against my will."

"Is that true?" I asked Newton.

"Afraid so," he replied.

"How will we get around this?" I asked. "Would a warrant issued by Smith & Wesson suffice?"

"I believe it might," he said.

Anne pulled the hammer back on the double-action revolver.

"Open the safe," she demanded.

"What if I refuse," said Miller. "You can't get your money if you can't get in."

"Thanks for confirming it's in there," said Newton.

"Shut up, copper," snapped Anne. Then turning to Miller "If you refuse, I'll shoot your secretary or, better still, I'll shoot you in the kneecap."

She lowered her aim point from his chest to his leg.

"Never really heals," I said, "You'll be walking with a cane for the rest of your life."

"Fine," said Miller. "I'll open it, but that won't solve either of our problems."

"It will go a long way to solving mine," she said.

Miller went to the safe, dialed the combination, pulled the lever, and opened the door. He gestured for Anne to look in. There was a manilla envelope. He pulled it out and showed her the money.

"Count it out loud," she said.

He did as he was ordered.

"Ten Grand. Now what?"

"Put the money back in the envelope and give it to me."

When she had the envelope, Anne ordered Miller and his secretary to stand next to us. She kept a sharp eye trained in our direction.

"My oh my. What ever am I going to do with the four of you?"

"If I counted right," I said, "you only have two bullets left. You used two on Teller and two on Newton. You could tie us all up and gag us, but that would be leaving four witnesses. I think you'll find the police much more thorough looking for a double-murderer than they normally are for confidence men. No, I'm afraid that won't do.

"You could shoot Newton and me and strike a deal with Miller. I'm sure his secretary could be convinced to keep her mouth shut."

"Yes," she said, her voice trembling with fear, "I won't say a word. Just don't hurt me please."

"Thanks for the excellent suggestion," said Newton, "remind me to thank you in the next life."

"But there's still a problem," I continued. "The cops already know you killed Teller, and when they pull the slugs out of us and match them, it won't matter what the other two have to say. That won't do either. What's a girl to do? Four witnesses and two bullets. Come to think of it, only one. I'm going to reach slowly into my pocket...nothing tricky...and show you something."

I extracted a .22 round, held it between my thumb and forefinger, and showed it to her.

"I took this out when you went to freshen up last night."

"Very clever, Lou, but you forget," she smiled, "there's still Newton's gun and it has six bullets."

"Listen up, Joan-of-Arc," she said to the secretary. "I want you to crawl over there," she said while gesturing with the barrel of her gun, find that pistol, and bring it to me. Don't try anything funny and get a hold of yourself for God's sake. Stop acting like a child."

"I'm afraid I can't do that," said a preternaturally calm voice as a gunshot rang out sending Anne sprawling backward. The secretary held a double shot derringer in both hands in perfect firing position.

"Four brothers, all cops," she said. "They worry about me. I keep it handy."

"Why didn't you use it earlier," I asked.

"I didn't have the opportunity, so I thought I'd play the helpless female until one presented itself. I was out of options at the end and decided to act."

"What's your name?" asked Newton.

"Mary Dunlop. Am I in trouble?"

"Hell no. I owe you a dinner."

I went and checked on Anne. She would be all right, at least until the state sent two thousand volts through her.

Newton gave Mary the number to the precinct and asked her to dial it for him. She did so and brought him the phone. He got the desk sergeant and asked for Gallo.

"Dom, it's Bill Newton. Send a team over to Miller's Lumber. We've got the perps who poisoned Jansen. One's a woman, she also shot Teller. She had the murder weapon on her. Shot me with the damn thing. Yeah, a couple of medics would probably come in handy. Yes, I said a couple. The dame got winged too. Get moving."

He hung up and returned the phone to Mary. He asked her to tend to Anne, who was seated on the floor with her back against the desk. He had me pull two chairs over and put Anne in one. He ordered Miller to take the other.

"You're both under arrest for the murder...make that the attempted murder of Victor Jansen."

"You've got nothing that ties me to anything," said Miller. "What's unusual about a businessman having ten thousand dollars in his office safe. This woman is a career crook and liar. My attorney will impeach her without breaking a sweat. They'll laugh you out of court."

"I'll let the DA figure that out. I collect the garbage; he brings it to the dump."

"Bill," I said. "You might want to check in that envelope. Could be something interesting in there."

Chapter 34

We were in the Emergency Room. Bill was dressed only in his skivvies as he sat on the edge of an examination table. A doctor, who didn't look old enough to vote, probed inside the gunshot wound with a pair of forceps. Bill winced in pain.

"Watch it, sonny. That hurts."

"Almost there, Lieutenant. Hang on," he answered.

He extracted the forceps and dropped a slug into a pan adjacent to the bed. Then he stitched up the wound.

"You're lucky," he said, "it didn't hit anything important. The nurse will be in shortly to dress the wound. You'll be a little sore for a week, but then you'll be good as new."

When we were alone in the room, Bill gave me a hard stare.

"How'd you know there was ten grand in that safe, and while we're at it, how'd you know about the two notes in the envelope?"

"If you retract the questions, I won't have to lie to you."

He thought about it for a moment and changed subjects.

"What was your plan if Mary hadn't been packing that popgun? You couldn't have been counting on that."

"Simple, Anne only had one bullet. I was hoping she'd shoot you first."

"What a pal."

"I was just trying to get her thinking about her situation, maybe confuse her. The longer I kept her talking, the more opportunity I'd have to catch her off guard and charge her. I couldn't let her get your gun; I was on the verge of charging her when Mary came to the rescue. Not much of a plan but it was all I had."

"These arrests," said Bill, "aren't going to take the heat off me. As far as the suits and the press are concerned, it's still the shooting they want solved. All we've done is eliminate two suspects. The skirt and the father."

"We still have two Millers left. Could be the right hand didn't know what the left was doing. One of them might have hatched their own plot. Junior was afraid Jansen might displace him at the company. Maybe he also has a note. As for Mercedes, who knows what she's capable of. Roz said she was acting peculiarly."

"Why would she go through with the wedding if she knew the groom was a fraud?"

"I think it really was love, or maybe she felt she could change him. How many women have sold themselves that chunk of baloney? The fact remains the only way Jansen could guarantee his safety was to spring the extortion close to the wedding. Jansen declared early, putting himself in the crosshairs. He was too much of a pro to make such a foolish mistake. He had to figure Anne would try to sour the deal or Miller would have him disposed of. He needed to come clean with Mercedes before her father got wise. That way he was inoculated should Anne rat him out. He'd let Mercedes take it from there with daddy."

"Which means we can eliminate Mercedes as a suspect."

"Not necessarily," I said.

Our conversation was cut short by a nurse. She went about the business of dressing Bill's wound. She didn't have much to say until she was done.

"That should do it," she said.

We thanked her. As she was leaving, she almost collided with Detective Gallo who was entering.

"You doing okay, boss?" he asked. "We heard Sam Spade here nearly got you killed."

"That's enough of that, Dom. You get our two crime scenes tidied up?"

"Clean as a whistle. Miller's in the slammer, and the dame is down the hall handcuffed to her bed. Just to let you know, Miller's mouthpiece is already trying to spring him. DA is worried we've got nothing to tie him to the dame."

"But you do," I said, "Kowalczyk, the Blacksmith."

"That two-bit punk? What's he got to do with this?" asked Gallo.

"You know him?" Asked Bill.

"Yeah, a bottom-feeder and muscle-for-rent. We've collared him a dozen times…all petty stuff. He's harmless."

I held up the cast on my right hand.

"Not that harmless," I corrected. "He connects the arsenic to Teller and the dame. Teller connects to Miller. The DA will be a happy man."

"Pick him up, Dom," said Newton.

Before Gallo left, Bill read him in on everything that had happened. He left out the part about my amazing clairvoyance concerning the contents of the safe in Miller's office. It was swell of him.

An orderly came in and asked if I was Lou Rizzo.

"Yeah, how'd you know it was me?"

"The lady on the phone said you had an eyepatch, a cast on your left arm, and were probably in with Lt. Newton. I figured the rest out by myself. The phone is at the nurse's station down the hall."

I thanked him, told Bill I'd be right back, and headed to the phone. The head nurse was busy, but the receiver was off the hook and lying on her desk. I picked it up.

"Rizzo," I said.

"Lou, it's Roz. Are you all right? I got a call you were in a shoot-out."

"I'm fine, but Bill got nicked up a little. He'll probably get cited for courage or be fired. It's always a fine line with the Brass. Same thing in the Air Corps. You at the office?"

"Yes."

"Do me a favor and grab three Reubens from *Nestor's* and see if you can scare up three bottles of beer. We'll be there in about an hour and we're going to solve a murder."

"Okay, I'll be waiting."

"Did I hear you right?" asked Bill who had followed me down the hall

I nodded and smiled.

"And here's some more good news. It's my turn to buy."

Chapter 35

"Let's stop by and see Anne Purcell or whatever her name is," I said.

"Good idea. I've got a few questions for her," said Newton as he struggled to pull up his pants with only one hand, the other arm being too painful to move. Between the two of us, we finally got him presentable and stepped back out into the hall. We could see a uniformed cop guarding the entrance to a room near the end of the corridor.

The uniform at the door saw us approaching, recognized Newton, and snapped to attention. Bill acknowledged him with a wave, and we both strode in. She was sitting upright with her right arm in a sling, her left handcuffed to the bedrail. According to the attending nurse, she had taken a slug in her right bicep. Derringers aren't very accurate, but Mary's had been accurate enough.

"Could you excuse us a moment, honey," said Newton while flashing his badge.

When we were alone, he began questioning her.

"What's your name?" he asked.

"I'm not talking to you, copper. Get me a lawyer."

"Listen up, sister. We've got you dead to rights. You're either going to fry or go to jail for the rest of your life. Your cooperation will probably be the deciding factor."

"I'm not going to get the chair. The state won't execute a woman, especially one that looks like me. Once I start laying it on thick on the stand, anything can happen. Teller was self-defense. No one can tie me to the arsenic except a street hood. The only testimony you can get that puts me anywhere near the victim before the wedding is from an alcoholic private dick who raped me in my hotel room." Bill gave me a sideways glance.

"It's a long story," I said.

"Then," she continued, "you have this problem; the victim died of a gunshot. The worst you could get me on is attempted murder. So, until you can offer me a better deal, I've got nothing to say"

"I'll ask again, what's your name and where are you from?"

She smirked and said nothing.

"She's from the Cleveland area. Grew up an Indians fan. Have your colleagues up there do some digging. I have an associate who knows a lot of people in the trade. He's working that angle as we speak. He'll come up with something sooner or later."

When we were about to leave, she surprised us both. "Can I get a minute alone with Rizzo?"

Bill looked from me to her then back at me.

"Sure," he said, "I'll wait outside."

"What's this all about?" I asked.

"When did you get wise to me?"

"Almost from the beginning. I thought, here's a dame who's spent her whole life chasing down the big payoff. There's no profit in revenge; you had to be working another angle. I didn't know what that was, but I knew eventually you'd reveal yourself. Once I gave you Teller, you had all you needed and fired me. That was a bad play. You should have just disappeared. I didn't figure on you plugging him, but he was no saint and was going down as an accessory to Jasen's murder anyway. You saved the state the cost of a trial."

"See you in court," she said.

Chapter 36

Roz was waiting for us at the office. She handed both of us a sandwich wrapped in wax paper soaked through with grease. I took the chair behind my desk. Bill and Roz sat on the opposite side like attentive students.

"The suspense," said Bill, "is killing me, Lou. What have you got?"

"Don't you want to eat first?"

"Quit messing with me. I've been on a thousand stakeouts. I can do both."

"A nice cold one would loosen my tongue. What do say, Roz?"

She produced three cold bottles of Schlitz and a bottle opener. The bottles were sweating condensation. I popped the top on mine and took a swig. Delicious. I unfolded the wax paper, grabbed my sandwich with two hands, took a bite, and chased that with another swig. I asked Roz to grab the police photos and the newspaper account. I selected the broader of the two shots taken in the loft and set the others aside with the paper.

"The answer to this mystery," I began, "has been here all the time. We just needed a few little details to make the whole thing fit. These photographs always struck me as all wrong, but I couldn't put my finger on exactly why."

"Take this photograph," I said pointing to the taped outline where Abigail Clayborn was found. "She claims the guy she identified as the shooter came up behind her and covered her mouth with an ether-soaked handkerchief. If that's what happened, what's her body doing six feet away? The shooter had to drag her over there. Again, the question is why?"

"Now, look at the organ bench. For her body to be moved six feet, the shooter had to drag her like this..."

I came around the desk, positioned myself behind Roz, and put my arms across her chest.

"Dragging her backwards over the bench would mean that her legs would go over last. That would probably tip the bench over, but at the very least, would cause it to move. But if we look at the photo, it is perfectly square with the organ. Add to that, ether acts fast but not instantaneously. There would have been a brief struggle, but her hat and purse are still sitting undisturbed on the bench. There's no sign of any physical activity at all. Another question. Why did the killer elect to bring the handkerchief and the vial with the body? It would have been easier to just drop them by the bench."

"I see where you're going," said Bill, "but for now it's all circumstantial."

"You're right it is, but this next part isn't. How could the killer have known that Clayborn would be the lone occupant of the loft? He couldn't assume the soloist would call in sick, which, by the way, she wasn't. I spoke to her on the phone. She claimed Clayborn called her the night before to tell her that her services wouldn't be needed."

"You're saying Clayborn assisted the shooter," said Bill.

"No, said Roz," as the lightbulb went on in her head. "He's saying she is the shooter! Where's that newspaper story?"

I smiled as she took the scent. I handed her the copy of the *Globe.*

"Look closely at this shot of her being carried out. Notice anything unusual?"

He stared at it for a while, then exhaled heavily in frustration. "Break out the dunce cap, I'm stumped."

"She's wearing white lace gloves that match her purse and hat. She claims she was at the organ getting ready to play a hymn. Nobody plays with their gloves on, but they'd come in handy if you didn't want to leave prints on a murder weapon."

"Then there are those mysterious binoculars...," I began.

"I got this one," said, Bill. "If her story is going to hold up, she needs a patsy to hang it on. It can't be a guest or anyone else people would notice. She uses the binoculars to scan the peanut gallery and sees poor old Jake Carlson from Corn Pone, Iowa standing by himself. She notices he has a slight limp...a nice touch. Bingo, she fingers him as the shooter.

"It went like this," he continued. "She brings a vial of ether and a man's handkerchief to the loft railing. She lines up the shot and kills Jansen. The place erupts, all eyes turn toward the loft, but she goes to her hands and knees and is invisible behind the railing. She slides the rifle across the wooden floor, through the entry, and gravity takes it to the first landing. Then she drugs herself. Maybe she's unconscious, maybe not. That's how the cops find her. How am I doing?"

"Head of the class," I said.

"Wouldn't she be concerned that someone might smell ether on her gloves?" asked Roz.

"She probably figured no one would check. Even if they did, she could claim her hand went to her face in self-defense," I said.

"What did she have against Jansen?" asked Roz.

"Damn good question," added Bill. "You said she was having trouble making ends meet. Maybe someone made an offer.

"That's a good motive," I replied, "but it's wrong. This wasn't about money. It was a crime of passion."

"Guess you better give me back that dunce cap. I'm not following you."

"I'm not either," said Roz.

"Our whole perspective on this case has been based on a faulty assumption which caused us to view any evidence from a flawed point of view. We all assumed it took a good shot to hit Jansen from that distance. But it wasn't a good shot; it hit the wrong man. She was aiming at Reverend Fletcher.

"I think if you grill Fletcher and work the staff gossip angle, you'll find they were an item."

"They were," said Roz. "Remember when I said I was going to interview for the choir director position? My real purpose was to sniff around and see what I could turn up. I asked the congregation secretary and bookkeeper why the last director left. They exchanged knowing looks, and the secretary said in a conspiratorial whisper that it was a personal relationship with the pastor gone wrong. Sounds like it might be this Sophie Fromm Lou spoke to."

"Why would she think she could make a shot like that in the first place?" asked Bill.

"Her deceased husband was an outdoorsman, and she said they often went hunting together. She knew her way around guns, but an M-1 is a heavy weapon for a woman. Add to that, shooting a human is a whole lot different than shooting game. All the practice in the world can't simulate the first time you try to pull the trigger on a man. She probably was more comfortable with a lighter rifle like a .22. Good for varmints and small game, like the rifle that was used to ambush Roz and me. If a smart cop got a warrant, I bet he'd find a gun case with a .22 that he may be able to tie to that incident. Might even be a space where an M-1 used to be stored."

"Why would she pick such a dangerous setting with such a high probability of failure?" asked Bill.

"Who can say, but jealousy is a dangerous emotion once it gets its tentacles around you. Maybe she couldn't think of a better plan. Maybe she wanted the drama, or maybe a part of her wanted to fail. I'm no shrink. The fact remains, there is no other way to fit the puzzle pieces together."

Bill studied his fingernails for a moment, then said, "Can I borrow your phone; I've got to make a few calls."

Chapter 37

It took a while for the dust to settle, and with it, public interest faded away. Faced with overwhelming evidence, the woman I knew as Anne Purcell was cooling her heels in jail awaiting trial. She refused to give up Miller, who remained free on bail. The Blacksmith had vanished, and the smart money said it was for good. With both he and Teller dead, there was no direct connection to the crime as long as Anne kept her mouth shut. The ten thousand dollars could be explained away, but the two typed notes were going to be a problem for him. Rumor had it the DA was trying to get Mercedes to flip on her old man. The scuttlebutt was if all else failed, his defense was going to be based on the claim that he couldn't be convicted of killing a dead man, but that still left attempted murder.

Abigail Clayborn was also in jail waiting for the DA to figure out what to charge her with: murder, attempted murder, or manslaughter. Her public defender, fresh out of law school, sat by while she confessed to shooting Jansen and trying to kill me that night outside my office. She was a sad case. If she found a halfway decent mouthpiece, she might be able to throw herself on the mercy of the court.

Mercedes Miller went into seclusion, refusing to speak with her father. She steadfastly maintained she and Jansen were in love. Odd as that might seem from the outside, there was no evidence to suggest otherwise. Her brother was now running Miller's Lumber and those in the business community agreed that it was just a matter of time before he ran it into the ground. In his office, in a stack of letters he hadn't gotten around to opening, the cops found a typed note identical to the second note sent to Senior.

I was sitting in our usual booth at the *Warning Track* waiting for Bill to arrive. It was quite a show when he finally did. There was a smattering of congratulatory applause and a gauntlet of back-slapping as he made his way across the room. Fellow cops grabbed his hand or offered a thumbs-up, a far cry from the last time we were here.

He took off his suit jacket, tossed it on the bench, loosened his tie, and slid in.

"Can you believe this nonsense?" he said.

"All hail the conquering hero," I replied. "You bagged three murderers and broke up a confidence scheme. The press says you're the greatest detective since the *Thin Man*. You own this town, pal."

"Humph, that's one way to look at it," he said while holding up two fingers to the waiter. "The mayor is embarrassed that I'm putting away one of his buddies. That means the commissioner will distance himself from me, as will the chief. They'll give me a citation because the press will demand it. Then it's back to the salt mines. I don't give a damn. I've got a year to go until I can chuck it all."

Our beers arrived and we toasted politicians, bureaucrats, and retirement. We each took a healthy pull.

"You know, Lou, I don't feel right accepting these accolades. You're the guy who cracked the case while I get all the credit in the press."

"Forget about it, Bill. I lied to you and almost got you canned. Besides, I got paid, that's all that matters."

"You did?"

"Yup, Anne paid me in advance. Ironic, isn't it."

"Sure is."

"Did you ever get anything useful out of Abigail Clayborn."

"That dame's wacko, lot's of loose screws rattling around in her toolbox. Revenge was her motive, but her method was pure madness. Turns out Reverend

Fletcher promised to marry her, then threw her over for...you had it right...Sophie Fromm. They were doing the horizontal waltz. I asked her why she didn't dust Fromm instead. She said she wasn't the one that betrayed her.

"When we searched her house, we found her husband's hunting rifle, a Remington 721 with a scope, a beautiful weapon. Why didn't she choose the better gun? Get this, she had a sentimental attachment to it. Couldn't bear ditching it at the crime scene. She knew her .22 wouldn't do, so she chose the M-1.

"She knew the weapon was unwieldy for a woman, but she practiced with it and felt confident she could make the shot. She was wrong. Her only regret is she missed. She takes comfort in the fact the scandal will ruin him. Like I said, wacko."

"You have to admit her plan had elements of genius, and she did have us all fooled. She almost pulled it off. It's always the little details that blow it up," I said.

Our conversation was interrupted when the background buzz in the room came to a halt. We heard a few whistles and turned to see Roz making her way towards us grinning like she just hit a twenty-to-one shot at the track. She was looking particularly fetching, decked out in a belted maroon number set off by matching heels and a gold necklace.

"Good evening, gentlemen. May I join you?"

"Since I invited you," I said, "I'd be a heel to say no. Do you mind, Bill?"

"The best thing that's happened to me all day."

Roz gave him her big-league smile; the one usually reserved for Picker. She'd been on a high since we broke the case, relishing the part she had played.

"I hear you did some impressive undercover work," said Bill. "You might have a future private eye on your hands, Lou."

Roz blushed like a schoolgirl. "Have you ordered yet?"

"We were just about to order a couple of sandwiches. Shall we make it three," asked Bill.

"Sandwiches? Lou said we'd be drinking wine

and dining on *Linguine Alle Vongole* at *Pasquale's*."

"Why would he say that?"

"Something about it being your turn to buy."

Thank you for reading The Twice Dead Groom. If you enjoyed it, you might want to try the first book in the Lou Rizzo series, Rizzo's Rules, available in the Amazon Store in both Kindle and paperback formats.

www.ingramcontent.com/pod-product-compliance
Lightning Source LLC
Chambersburg PA
CBHW072009170726
47999CB00014B/1401